W9-DIY-588

Life, Death and Tribulations by JAK

Life, Death and Tribulations by JAK

Just Another Kid

Tom Prange

iUniverse, Inc.
New York Lincoln Shanghai

Life, Death and Tribulations by JAK
Just Another Kid

iUniverse books may be ordered through booksellers or by contacting:

iUniverse
2021 Pine Lake Road, Suite 100
Lincoln, NE 68512
www.iuniverse.com
1-800-Authors (1-800-288-4677)

ISBN-13: 978-0-595-33993-8 (pbk)
ISBN-13: 978-0-595-78819-4 (cloth)
ISBN-13: 978-0-595-78781-4 (ebk)
ISBN-10: 0-595-33993-X (pbk)
ISBN-10: 0-595-78819-X (cloth)
ISBN-10: 0-595-78781-9 (ebk)

Printed in the United States of America

Throughout the course of time there are those who live life and those who know what it means to be alive. Throughout our time here on Earth we question our existence and fail to see the point. The point is that there is no real point to life but to live it to the fullest and make it so that there is nothing that can bring you down. People spend their whole lives in search for the reason of life when the answer is right there in front of them. Life is what you make it to be. It's up to you to decide..

CONTENTS

CHAPTER 1

MY NAME IS JAK

Just Another Kid

Don't smile at me
You judge people by what you see

What do you know
You just shrug your shoulders and say so

Don't lie to yourself
You just care about getting praise and wealth

But tell me have you looked at anyone else in the world
Or do you just look for those pearls

There is so much more
Things that you refuse tot look for

You don't care about the things around you
Yet there are many others just like that, too

Don't be too excited
'Cause you're "Just Another Kid"

Don't smile when you look at me
Because it is only you that you see

Have you ever thought of death as a funny thing? It's an interesting concept, don't you think? I mean, so many of us have this kind of fear of death, but do we actually know what it means? My guess would be that the answer would be "No" for most people. After all, we're only human. We're just these creatures who have this belief that we are the best, the greatest of God's creations. Truth be told, we may be great in so many ways, but there are still so many ways that we aren't.

I have a question for you. If we are so great, then why is it that we die? Shouldn't that be proof enough that we aren't as great as we have set ourselves to believe? You can say we are all just pieces on a checker board, and that board is this Earth that we live on. We all strive to reach the other side so we can become, in our view, these invincible things. We can move all across the board and do pretty much anything we wish. Yet what we don't realize is that we can still be defeated. Not only that, but sooner or later this game, like all things, must come to an end. When that time comes we will just be put back into our boxes and lose that greatness we strive so hard to get for ourselves. So then I ask, what is the point of it all?

The story I'm about to convey onto you shall answer that question. They're no little ponies or munchkins running around. There's no happy ending, for not everything ends in such a way. When it comes to something such as life, sometimes the ending is no jubilee. No, for if I was to concede to such a thing then I wouldn't do my story justice. I am one to speak only the truth, and truth I shall speak.

I guess if I were to actually begin to tell such a story as mine, I would be obligated to start where it all basically began. In this particular story the beginning is the same as all human's beginnings, birth. I was born in Southern Maine as Jake Benjamin Davis. It was January 30, 1987 and to the delight of Mr. Joseph M. Davis and Mrs. Linda P. Davis I was born. Despite being given the name Jake, my parents tended to refer to me as Jak. I became so accustomed to the name that I would actually use it in identifying myself.

I lived there for about three years. I enjoyed my life there, even if it was but a short time of my existence. I mean most kids love the first place where they live. It holds a special place in their hearts. When I was four, though, something I wasn't expecting occurred. You see my parents had come to the conclusion that it would be better for the family if they were to separate. How a parent can inform their child of such a thing I will never be able to contemplate, for there is no good way to say it.

It was decided that I was to live with my mother. We moved to southern New York a couple of miles away from New York City. I was five at the time. When you're a child of a single parent who has to work two to three jobs just to support a family, I guess you have no choice but to grow up a little faster than the other kids your age. It's almost like it's one of those written laws that states that you have to grow up. It just sucked. There's no other word, beyond vulgarity, that I can use to describe the situation.

The town we moved into was country like you could say. There were a lot of trees and woods. There weren't many stores or malls you could go shopping at either. Indeed I felt as if the town was a cheep knock off from *It's A Wonderful Life.* Everyone knew each other, even if they didn't want to. There was nothing you could do that the person standing next to you in line at the local gas station wouldn't hear about, or already knew. Everyone knew your life story and then some.

For entertainment I usually went exploring through the woods, so I wouldn't draw attention to myself. It may seem a little bit peculiar, but I always would hope that I'd find something amazing, like a hidden treasure left behind by some old Spaniard. I never did find much, but it was the mystery and fascination that maybe I would come across something that kept me searching. If anything it was usually a good walk. I'd occasionally find a nice spot, usually high up with a great view, before sundown and watch the sunset.

They're few things in this world that I believe are more beautiful and outstanding than a sun set. Just sitting and gazing upon that giant yellow ball of flame, as it slowly sets in that crisp blue sky as it shines down on everything. It was all I ever needed to brighten up my day. It's something that no one should live life without seeing. Looking up as the sky lights up in a billion different colors. It was as if the sky was dancing while on fire, and there you were, watching it burn in all its glory. It's just one of those *"must see"* things to me. Watching the sunset was one of the only things I could do and truly be happy about when ever I did it. It was just the world, and little old me during that time. It was an amazing feeling that I wished I could have had all the time. It was a time that I could smile form ear to ear, an actually mean it. It was in one word, *happiness.* That happiness, which much like many others, I didn't have enough of in my life. Yet, I had this understanding that I would never achieve it fully.

We moved into a fairly small house, but I guess it was pretty good for a family of two. The house I believe was about forty feet by forty feet and was two stories high. It had a small kitchen with a white tiled floor and a flower patterned wallpaper. Then there was a living room. It was all made out of wood, which made it look really nice in my view. I think it was oak, I'm not quite sure, but I do know that it had a large window that looked out into the street.

There was another room that my mom had transformed into her studio. The studio was only cleaned the first day my mom finished it. After that it became covered with all her "projects". In other words, things she was building to sell, but never really finished. She would always tell me she would finish them, but ultimately she never did. Then there was her room. It was a small room that fit her twin size bed, nightstand with a lamp on it, and a small black-and-white TV. That was the whole downstairs. I never really did go downstairs much I must say. I spent must of my time in the best room of the house. That would be upstairs in my room, which was the attic.

The attic wasn't that big, it was about the size of the living room so I guess it was fifteen feet by fifteen feet. The ceiling was in an arc, which I always thought was pretty cool. I had my bed in a corner, a desk across from the bed and a small color TV at the foot of my bed. I also had a bookshelf against a wall, which wasn't very crowded. I'll admit that I never was much into reading when I was younger so I never really bothered to get many books. I also had a little boom box near my bed. I really didn't use it that much until I was in junior high.

My room I guess you can say was my escape from the world outside. Some kids read, others write, some hang out with friends, and others do drugs or anything to waste time. For me, I'd go up to my room. I'd get a CD out, put it into the stereo, sit or lay on my bed, and listen to the music and reflected. What would I reflect upon you may ask? I liked to reflect on things that happened either on a certain day or as far back as I could remember. I'm betting you believe me to be a very odd person. I guess you could think that, but it worked for me.

My dad would visit every other weekend from Maine. My parents would always try and hide their dislike for one another. I guess they didn't want to make things harder for me than they already were. Unfortunately I was far smarter then they had given me credit for. I could tell just by the way they looked at each other. I comprehended that dislike they had for each other. You know that look a parent gives you when you've done something bad, like steal something or get caught drunk? Well the look they gave each other was ten times worse. I knew they were trying to not let me know, but I think by doing that they only made things seem so much worse.

Life isn't a fairy tale, and I had to grasp onto that concept pretty quick. Not everything has a happy ending. For if that was the case, then my parents would have been together, and we would have been the happiest family in the entire world. Nope, this is the real world my friend. One must be prepared for such disappointment, because if you're not, you're just going to be sucked into a spiral of pain heading headfirst to the ground.

I never let them, or anyone for that matter, know I was hurting inside. I knew I was depressed, but I would never allow another to know that. To me, showing emotion was a sign of weakness. If I were to show weakness, then the world would destroy me. Though, when I was alone in my room, and no one else was there, I would just look up at the ceiling. Just staring at it and listen to the guitar riffs echo from the stereo. Then, not realizing it, a tear would begin to drip down my check. Now I didn't go into a full-blown crying fest. No, that just wasn't me. It would just be three or four tears, but with every tear it felt like a hundred tears. It's hard to explain.

My mom didn't notice it at all really, which I was glad about, mostly because she was working two jobs to keep food on the table and a roof over our heads. She couldn't have taken notice to it. Usually after a day of hard work she would serve dinner and then go to her room and drink. I guess you could say my mom was an alcoholic. I didn't see it that way to tell you the truth. I knew my mom was hurting and that was just her way of dealing with things. So I accepted it. She was all I really had since my dad only came every other weekend.

When my dad came up we both knew that we had grown so apart over the years. We knew it was because of not seeing each other as much as a father and son should. It was kind of like meeting someone for the very first time. You'd say hi, tell them your name, ask them what they like and make pointless small talk. That was basically how it was with my dad. We were strangers from two different worlds. Sad don't you think? Not really knowing your own father, but that was just the way things worked out for me. I didn't have a choice in the matter, nor could I really have changed it. If I did things would have been a lot different.

"Family," isn't it an interesting word? It's a word accepted all across the world. Yet we as humans take it for granted. It isn't until we actually lose that family that we come to the realization of the importance of having a family. That's probably why I kind of characterize myself as lucky. I had lost my family at a young age. Unlike others, I didn't get the chance to grasp an understanding of the word "family." I am also in a way, very unlucky. Not knowing that word made me, in so many ways, cold inside. Like a stone, with no real feelings to show. I was in a way hidden beneath this shell that I had built around myself. As I got older that stone would go through some pretty rough courses and break, but ultimately it would keep reforming again and again until it had completely covered my life.

When we first moved into our new home our neighbors came over and greeted us into the neighborhood. I stayed up in the attic pretending to be asleep so I didn't have to talk to anyone. I didn't want to be seen by anyone really. To be honest, in a way I wished I were still back in Maine in my old house with my dad. I wanted mom to be there and then we could be a family again. We'd go to Disney World or something, laugh and just have fun. Then I could look at them, smile and know that this would last forever. That was my family.

Yet I knew that those thoughts were just that, thoughts. Everything had changed and I could do nothing to stop or change it. You know how it is don't you? You grow up thinking your family is amazing and it's going to last for ever and ever. Nothing can destroy it. Then one day you wake up and your whole world has been flipped upside down. That strong family is nothing more than a thing of the past. Your reality is that you are being juggled between your mom and dad. Your family is two weak ones instead of one strong one. You begin thinking why is this happening, why now, why me? Truth be told, there really isn't an answer to those questions. Sometimes things happen that we may not deserve or understand. The thing is that we can't do anything about it. We can blame God, but what good is that? We really can't blame anyone, and that includes ourselves. We aren't to blame and neither are our friends and family. Things just sort of happen, that's just the fact of it all. We may not like it, but we still can't control it. You just learn to deal with it. I wanted it all to go away. Just disappear and never be seen again.

As I lay on my bed, I listened as all of our new neighbors greeted my mom. All I wanted to do was scream as loud as I could. I hoped that everyone would just go away then. I wanted to scream and just fade away into the nothingness that I felt inside. I couldn't take dealing with everything that was going on. Everything was changing so fast around me. It was almost like the whole world was moving a hundred miles per hour, and there I stood. Just standing there and watching as everything zoom right by me. I was the tortoise and the world was the hare. The thing was, though, I wasn't going to win this race. I could try as hard as I could, but the fact was that I would never win. It wasn't really fair in my view, but like I've been saying, I'm just another human in this big world. A human wanting answers.

After what felt like eternity to me, everyone in our neighborhood that had come over to greet us finally left our new home. That just left my mom and me. There was no more talking like, "So where did you come from?" or "Where is your husband?" or any other stupid questions like that coming from the downstairs. I finally decided to go downstairs and rejoin my "new world."

My stomach was talking to me. I was pretty hungry after staying upstairs for most of the day after all. So I made a beeline straight for the kitchen. I mean after all, I was a growing five-year-old at the time and I needed some food to keep up with my growing body. My mom looked at me as I walked into the kitchen and laughed. "I see you've finally got out of bed Mr.," she joked as I opened the refrigerator door and pulled out a slice of ham.

"I needed something to eat," I replied. I got myself a bowl of cereal and sat at the table. My mom and I didn't talk much then, not really much to talk about. I guess that was why.

When I finished I went back upstairs to my room. I turned on the TV and watched some shows that were on, well tried. I never really enjoyed watching TV all that much. I soon got up and walked to my window. I looked out my window down at the street. There on the street some of the neighborhood kids were running around yelling and cheering. You don't know how much I wished I were out there playing with them. Just to feel the breeze of the wind in my hair as I ran back and forth across the street. It wasn't going to happen. Not because it just wouldn't, but more of because I refused to let it happen. It's hard to put in words. I guess the best way of explaining it is that moving away from my dad really affected me. At first it didn't, but when I had finally realized that this was it and that there was no going back. The family I had dreamt would stay together forever was in fact, finished and was a thing of the past. So I felt that if I actually joined those kids outside I would be losing everything back where my dad was and I didn't want to lose that. Joining them would just seal the deal and any hope I had put in my mind of things going back to the way they were before the whole separation would just disappear. My hopes would be destroyed. Then things would never be normal again. Why did it have to work out like that was all that I could ask? I could never figure out the answer.

You know how you may argue with someone you care about? You may not always agree with what they do with their lives, especially if it affects you personally. The bottom line, though, is that if you truly care about someone enough, and I mean care about him or her, then you will do anything you can to try and keep them and help them through their troubles. Even if it hurts you the bottom line is that it shouldn't matter. That person means everything to you. That's how it was with my dad and me. I thought I was losing him everyday and I didn't want that to happen and especially not then. It felt almost as if I wasn't ready to lose him. No kid should grow up without a mom or dad I believed, and I still believe that. While having one of them is still good it just wasn't the same really for me. Some people have only one parent for some reason and they're happy about it. It just wasn't like that for me. So I just kept asking myself, why is this happening to me? Why can't I have what every kid deserves?

Unfortunately this was just one of those things I would have to wait and see what would happen. My parents in a sense I guess separated for my sake, if you can comprehend that? You see they knew that things weren't really going to work out between them. So they figured that if they had stayed together, it wouldn't be all that fair to me. They wanted me to have better then that, thus, they separated. I'd get over it as the years went by, but I remember just caring about it so much back then. I was a young child who wanted the family he use to have returned back to normal. I felt like that family had been taken away from me far too soon. I'd never get it all back, and for some reason as the years went on, I began to not care about it so much. That's because I created a family of my own. That family consisted of my friends.

Chapter 2

Welcome To School And Growing Up

Friendship

Everyone has one, but do they know them
Our friends mean everything to us we say
So we never think that they're not going to be there one day

It's sad but oh so true
It seems like it will last forever
But then forever seems like never

So look at your friend
Look into their eyes
And don't say any lies

You are friends
That means something

It's more valuable than any golden ring

Tell your friend that
Because it's more important than love
For know that friendship is as beautiful as a dove

You must act quick
For if one is to wait
Then one is trying with fate

I remember my first time stepping into my Elementary School. It was my first day of kindergarten. It was like stepping into a whole New World. All I had known was the inside of my house. I didn't really go out all that much. I was kind of a hermit, you could say, who would stare aimlessly out of the window. The sun shone down upon the black nicely paved road where all the neighborhood kids would engage in a game of tag or other games. It looked like fun to me, but I never went out to join. Besides the reason I talked about before, I also figured that they wouldn't want me to join. I always thought that way when it came to getting involved with other people. I could never join anything with out being pushed into it. Like a little kid who is up in line to sit on Santa's lap for the first time and needs a little push by his mom or dad to go up.

My kindergarten class was like a dream world. It had six tables, four against the wall right by the window and the other two kind of floating in the middle of the room. The rug was a kind of dark red color that went pretty well with the blue colored walls. There were a couple of shelves with books in them and some with toys in them, which were more like building toys. I thought that school was pretty cool after seeing all of the toys.

My teacher was a skinny old lady. She had to be about five foot four I'm guessing, with long white hair. It was so white that to me it that it almost seemed like snow. She was wearing a dress that was green with yellow sunflowers all over it. This definitely didn't look all that good with her white hair. I'd have to say she was fifty or early sixties because her skin was wrinkly, but not too wrinkly. She was standing there when we entered and greeted my mom and I with a smile. "And what is your name?" she asked me in a gentle voice.

"My name is Jake," I replied as nicely as I could. You can understand I was kind of nervous being that this was my first day of school.

"Well Jake is there anything else you want to go by?" she asked. I just stared up at her in complete confusion. What did she mean anything else I go by? Was I going to have to change my name now that I was in school? I looked at my mom for some sign of help.

My mom smiled and said, "I usually just call him Jak for short."

"Okay," my teacher replied. "Well Jak my name is Mrs. Kenny and if you would like you can call me Mrs. K."

I nodded my head since I figured that was what I was expected to do. I almost felt like some kind of a puppet. Being lead by my strings to wherever I was told to go or say whatever I was directed to say.

"Well Jak," Mrs. K said to me, "go take a seat and wait until the rest of your class arrives."

At this I froze. I had feared this moment from the first time my mom told me I was going to school. The first seat, the seat that would ultimately determine the rest of my school career. The most important decision I'd make in school. What if no one wanted to sit next to me I thought? Then I'd be the loser of the class. I was sweating a little at this point because I had no idea what I should do.

I decided to go to the table in the corner by the window. I decided that was a good seat because if I did end up alone at least no one was behind me. Which meant no one could make fun of me behind my back. Another reason was because if I was alone I could always just turn and look out the window. This way I could try and avoid the reality of being the outcast, the lone wolf, the kid in the corner or anything that the kids in my class would characterize me as.

I was pretty mature for my age and I guess that was why I was so worried. If I wasn't I would have probably not have been worrying at all. I'd be too busy picking my nose to care. I wasn't like every other kid though, so I did worry. So there I sat sweating as if I was in some prison camp awaiting the bullets of the enemy troops to execute me. Hoping and praying that at least one person would sit at my table so I wouldn't be alone.

Slowly the rest of my class arrived. To my relief some kids actually sat at my table and not only that, they even talked to me. We talked about kid stuff, like the newest cartoon or toy. I was actually smiling, something I hadn't really done much of since my parents separated. It felt pretty good. For the first time I felt like I actually fit in with something in my life. It's one of the greatest feelings in the world. I'd ever dare say it was right there with a first kiss or getting married.

As the school year went on I enjoyed going to school more and more. I enjoyed it so much that on vacations I was probably the only kid in my class, let alone the school, who actually wanted to go back to school. It wasn't that I hated being home or anything like that. It was that I honestly loved being in school and learning. I loved spending time with my mom, but I wanted more from life. Kind of greedy, yes, but I didn't care all that much back then. I was five going on six and loving it like a fat kid at an all you can eat buffet.

With all of this talk about school, I'm drawn to discuss my best friend in school. Upon doing this I must come to the realization that in fact my best friend wasn't in school at the time that I became acquainted with him. In fact, he lived right next door to me. His name was Seth Tompson. He was a little younger than I was, but he was pretty cool. Due to our birthdays we were in different grades so he hadn't started school yet. Seth was a cool kid. He always did things his way rather then the way that others may have wanted him to do it. He, in a sense, was my role model, even if I was older than he was.

He was also, I guess you could say, a bad kid. That's only if one was to go by the standards we are all used to. He cursed, smoked, and drank. He was a regular bad ass I guess. For those who didn't know him he was as bad as they came. Yet to those who did know him, well, we all saw him in a totally differently way. No matter what Seth did we all could just look into his eyes and know he would always be there for us. Like a dog to his master, if one of us were in trouble he would appear and help us out. We were all his little Timmys, and he always was there to help us out of that well we had fallen into. He didn't have to ask if we needed help, he just would be there and help. He was the best friend I could have ever asked for.

Seth's brother Brad would hang out with us as well. He was two years older than I was, but it didn't matter. He was slightly heavy, but like we use to say, he was the big teddy bear. He had this messy curly hair that he would have to tie back so he could see. He wore these glasses that actually looked like he didn't have to wear. They looked like glass to me personally. Even when I put them on I could still see straight fairly well. We always said he was faking it. He'd just look at us and shook his head at that. I began to think back to that day that for the first time I met Seth and Brad. It was one day I wouldn't forget.

It was the first winter in our new house. My mom was at the store and I was outside in my back yard (one of my few adventures to the outside world at the time). I was rolling snow up trying to make my first snowman. I had just watched *Frosty the Snowman* and wanted to make a snowman for myself. As I rolled the snow I suddenly saw something fly over the fence from our neighbor's yard into my backyard. I then saw a brown hair kid wearing a big blue jacket and black jeans get tossed over my neighbor's fence into my backyard. The kid landed in the snow with a loud thud. He then began to slowly get to his feet. His face was cover with snow as he stood up. I just sat there behind the big snowball I had rolled and watched. He stood up and then wiped the snow off his face and looked around.

"Seth, you there?" I heard a voice say from the other side of the fence.

"Yeah I'm here," the boy that came over the fence said as he wiped the snow off his face. "How about next time you fucking get me over a little more gently?"

I just sat back in amazement. I had never heard someone my own age say something like that before. I looked at the kid and didn't recognize seeing him in school before going on winter break.

He looked around and exclaimed, "Wow, it's like I'm in another world. You should see this Brad."

"Well I don't have anyone to throw me over," the voice on the other side of the fence said.

"I just realized something," the boy in my yard exclaimed. "How the hell am I going to get back to the other side?"

There was a moment's pause followed by the word shit from both sides. The boy looked around and said, "Well at least I found our ball." The boy ran over to the ball and picked it up."

Suddenly he turned and saw me. We both just stared at each other. Then we both screamed. The boy yelled, "Brad help there's an alien over here. He's going to eat me."

I could hear feet running and a door open and close to a house from the other side of the fence.

I look at the kid in my yard and wondered what he was talking about and then I realized that in fact he was saying I was an alien. "I'm not an alien," I declared. "You are the alien."

"No I'm not!" the boy argued. "You are the alien!"

"No, you are!" I argued back.

"Oh yeah, well then what is that?" he exclaimed pointing to the beginning of the base of my snowman.

"That's my snowman," I replied.

"That's not a snowman," the boy exclaimed with a laugh.

I looked at the base and said, "Well I'm trying to make it. I just started." The boy walked over and began to examine the beginning of my snowman like he was some type of person who studies fine art.

"Well," he said, "it's a start. You're in luck though, cause I'm the bestest snowman builder in the world." A huge smile spread across his face and he said, "I could help you out here if you want?"

I looked at him and smiled, "Well I guess I could use the help." Suddenly the door to the fence opened and a lady walked in. A slightly chubby kid with curly black hair followed her in.

"What's going on," the lady asked.

"Nothing mom I'm okay. Hey, is it all right if I stay here for a little bit till we finish a snowman?"

The lady nodded her head and with that left me with the two boys. The boy that came over the fence looked at me and said "My name is Seth. This is my older brother Brad, he's in second grade."

"My name is Jake, but you can call me Jak," I told them.

"Well Jak, lets make the bestest snowman in the world," Seth said.

With that the three of us began working on our snowman. I can't really explain what I was feeling during this time. What I can tell you, though, is that it was one of those feelings you only feel at certain times in your life. The closest word I can use to describe the feeling is, well, joy. It was like having my first ice cream and just eating it feeling happy and looking at my parents, smiling, happy and together. I just couldn't stop smiling while we worked on our snowman.

As night began to fall over our small town we finished our snowman. It was about five feet tall. We found rocks for eyes, which sat right above the carrot we had placed for the nose. We then got an old hat and placed it on top of the snowman's head. We then found sticks to place as arms and a small stick that we made into the mouth of the snowman. We finished right as my mom was pulling up into the driveway in our busted up station wagon.

I ran over to her and gave her hug saying, "Mommy, mommy look what we made. We made an actual snowman. Isn't it the bestest snowman in the world?" My mom smiled at me then looked at Seth and Brad.

Seth waved and said, "My name is Seth and this is Brad. We're Jak's friends." I would never forget those words. It was the first time in my life that anyone had ever called me their friend. He was smiling, but I could tell he wasn't just smiling because he was happy. I could tell that he actually meant what he said about us being friends. I felt kind of tingly all over. It was like I was being tickled all over my body and I couldn't escape from smiling and just being happy. My mom suddenly pulled out a camera from her car.

"Jak go over to the snowman honey. All of you group around the snowman so I can take a picture," she said.

I ran over and Brad, Seth and I put our arms around each other and stood in front of the snowman. My mom raised the camera and said, "Everyone say cheese."

We gave our biggest smiles and made bunny ears behind each other's back. That was the beginning of Seth's, Brad's and my friendship. I took the picture and hung it in my room so that I would always remember that day. The first day, while being in my new town, that I was truly happy.

After we became friends, school became more fun for me. I always looked forward to recess. At recess Brad and I would play games of tag or pretend we were great adventurers and explore the playground. Things became even better the next year. Seth started school then, and the three of us would hang out. All our grades were pretty good. We all were smart for our ages in the sense that we could learn things faster than other people could in our grades. We just didn't apply ourselves all that much. I also began to meet new people and make new friends. I was breaking out of that shell that I had put myself in. I was free for the first time.

One of my other new friends was named Ron Henandez. He was in my grade. He was your normal skinny dirty blond hair kid. The thing that stood out most about him was this big grin he'd always get across his face. We use to call him Goofy because of his height and that grin of his. He lived right down the street from Seth, Brad and me. His parents were friends with Seth and Brad's parents and that was how we met and became friends.

Seth's family had a little party and my mom went. So that left Seth and me since Brad was at their aunt's house. We were bored out of our minds just sitting their listening to all the grown ups drink and talk. There's nothing more boring to an eight and seven year old then to sit and listen to grownups talk. It was like scratching nails on a chalkboard. Even when you know it's coming you still can't stand it. I was so bored that I wanted to just poke my eyes out. That's when we saw Ron.

I had seen him a couple of times before in school. He had a different teacher then me, but we had met before. Usually at lunch or recess we'd pass by each other. We didn't hang out or anything though. Seth was actually the one who called him over and introduced us to each other. It was kind of weird.

Seth just looked over and called Ron over. "Hey Ron," he said, "come here."

Ron came walking over to us. "Hi Seth," Ron replied.

"Hey," Seth said. "This is Jak, he's my friend next door. He's a real knuckle head, but he's cool when you get to know him."

"Hi," I waved.

"Hey," Ron waved back. Then there was complete silence. I think it's easier when you're older to continue a conversation. As a kid there isn't much to really talk about. In fact if it weren't for Seth the silence would have continued.

"Well this shit is boring," he declared. "Let's go outside, cause I can't stand it in here anymore."

Ron and I nodded our heads and we headed outside. It was a nice spring day. The sun hung high in the sky and the trees were beginning to sprout new leaves. Indeed spring was in the air.

As we stepped outside Ron looked at me and said, "You're in my grade aren't you?"

"Yeah," I answered, "I'm in Mrs. Kelly's class."

"I thought I had seen you before," Ron replied. We began to talk about school and what we liked to do. Seth entertained himself by climbing up a couple of trees. Looking back at our conversation now it must have been the must childish thing.

"You like transformer?" Ron asked.

I looked at him and my face nearly dropped. "Are you kidding," I exclaimed. "Transformers are the coolest."

We started talking about all the different kind of transformer and about our favorites. Both of us like Optimus Primal. He was a giant freight truck and would transform into this giant robot. He was awesome to me. Just the fact that Ron liked him as well made me like him even more. We ran to my house, grabbed all my transformers, brought them over to Seth's house, and we played with them.

Seth kind of just watched us. The thing with Seth was that he never really was a kid; or rather he never wanted to be one. He was so much older then the rest of us mentally. You know how I said I was different then other kids? Seth was just like that. The only difference was that I was still a kid at heart and strived to be that way. Seth on the other hand wanted more from life. To him being young was some kind of punishment placed upon him. If he were to ever embrace it then he'd be embracing defeat. Yet some how despite our different views we were friends and there was no one I felt closer to.

I guess that's why with Ron it was a different kind of friendship. Ron was that kind of kid I wanted to be at the time. No worries about life except the coolest toy or TV shows. I saw him as everything I wanted to be. Yet, I knew it could never be and I knew he'd never really understand me. Even when we were playing with my transformers I had this strange feeling. I knew we were so different. I wondered how someone like him and me could truly be friends. I was wrong though, as I usually am. As the years went on I really couldn't see myself not being friends with Ron. He became a part of my life, and more importantly, a part of me.

Since Ron was in my grade we hung out a lot in school and did work together in class. It is always nice having a friend close by, especially when trouble happens. Usually when trouble happens is when you can really see if your friends will always have your back in a tough situation. For that is the true test of friendship.

I remembered the first day I got in trouble in school. I was in fifth grade at the time. Ron and I were doing our group work when the class bully Henry McLarson came walking over. His little gang closely followed him. They stood a little ways away from us talking and laughing. Ron and I didn't pay much attention to them really. We were trying to finish our work. I had this strange feeling though, as if I knew something bad was about to take place.

After him and his group was done talking Henry came walking over to us with a big grin on his face. He was a relatively fat kid that had to be at least twice my size. I wasn't all that big when I was younger, which unfortunately forced me to look up to a lot of people. He had red hair and the freckles to match. He had these small beady eyes, which I thought were due to his fat cheeks, which would usually just glare around the class as if he was some kind of hawk, waiting for the right moment to strike his pray. Everyone had an understanding that he was deciding whom he was going pick on next. His teeth, which were by far the most atrocious feature on him, were yellow and showed exactly what he had eaten for lunch. His breath had a sour smell, much like that of a skunk that had been run over in the street on a hot summer day. Yeah, if there was one kid you didn't want coming up to you, Henry was that kid.

He looked down at Ron and me very smugly and asked, "What are you doing?" Just by the way that he said it made a red light flash in my head. I knew now without a shadow of doubt, something bad was about to take place.

"We're doing our work," Ron replied.

He didn't look up at Henry, but you could tell by his tone that he was a bit nervous.

Henry looked at our paper and said, "It looks like you did a lot." Suddenly he grabbed Ron's papers. "Thanks, now I can have my work finished too, losers," Henry snickered at Ron and me.

As he began to walk away I stood up quickly and snapped, "Give it back now or I'll tell."

That stopped Henry, which at the time I wasn't sure was a good thing. He glared at me, almost testing me. "Oh, is the poor little baby going to cry because I took his buddies papers?" Henry laughed.

His gang was laughing in the distance. He got up real close to me, so close that I could see the rolls on his faces. His breath pierced my nose like daggers but I refused to back down. He looked down at me with his eyes, which made me feel uneasy. It was like he was a cat, staring at his prey, waiting for me to make the wrong move so that he could make his move and attack. "Look you little dumb ass," he finally said, "since your daddy left and you're the only man in the house I'm going to leave you alone. After all, I wouldn't want to be the one to kill your mom's only man. It isn't like she can, or will ever get anyone else."

What happened next, I still can't believe happened. It was as if something exploded in me. I was like a rabid dog tearing up the first thing in front of me, and that thing was Henry. As he turned away and began walking I let out a yell and ran at him, tears streaming from my eyes and all. As he turned his pig like face towards me it was met by my angry fist. He stumbled back, but I wouldn't let up. I knew that if I did let up he would gain his composure and surely beat me. I tackled him and he tripped over a chair that was out. I was on top of him at this point and began unloading punches like a machine gun to his face. Suddenly a fist hit my face. I fell off Henry and saw that his gang was coming over to help him.

They really didn't get the chance to though. I thought for sure my life was about to be cut short, but the next thing I knew I saw Ron run right into the group knocking them down. Though Ron was skinny he was pretty tall. He was nearly as tall as Henry. I saw him swing his fist at the nearest gang member nailing them in the face. I quickly got up and began helping him. The fight would soon end though. My fifth grade teacher, Mrs. Ohorn had gotten help from some other teachers who were close by and they separated all of us. Henry was still lying on the floor of the classroom crying. My heart was pounding with in my chest as we were all dragged down to the principal's office, Mrs. Sokren.

Mrs. Sokren always seemed to be in a bad mood in my view. She had to be in her forties, but because her face was always wrinkled by a frown or stern look she looked like she had to be at least seventy or maybe even older than that. She looked around at all of us and began lecturing to all of us about how fighting was bad. All our parents were called and we spent the rest of our day in the office sitting. As I left school my mom was there to pick me up. She didn't look too happy. She had one of those looks that a parent usually has when their kid does something wrong. We walked to the car in complete silence. I didn't look up at her. I was like some sad dog walking to their dog-house because they chewed up their master's shoes and were being kicked out into the back yard.

As we pulled into the driveway my mom stopped the car and we just sat there. We were like soldiers awaiting the other's move. Finally my mom turned to me and said, "Well, what happened?" I suddenly felt calm. My mom didn't have the same tone in her voice that she would have had if she were angry. It was more of a kind of tone that made me think she was more concerned than angry. I then began to tell my mom the story of what happened. When I finished she just looked at me. Her green eyes just looked at me and it almost felt like she was in some way looking deep into my soul. She then opened her mouth and said, "Well I hope this doesn't happen again or at least that it doesn't become a daily thing." Then she smiled to my surprise and said, "At least you won the fight." I looked at my mom in total amazement and smiled. I loved my mom. I didn't get in as much trouble for the rest of my elementary career. Not even that much inmiddle school. Though, something happened at the end of middle school that would ultimately start to shape and change my life.

It was the summer before I was going to start to go to high school. I was with my friends like usual, but something was different this time. Maybe it was something in the air. I can't explain it but I knew something was going to happen, kind of like I was Spiderman and my spider sense was tingling. We were walking through the woods like we normally do. I was pretty pissed off due to the fact that my mom and I had just gotten into a fight. Why is it that those who we love most in this world always seem to hurt us the most? I guess it's because we love them so much that those little things that they do that hurt us seem to hurt us just a little bit more than they are actually suppose to hurt.

My mom had been drinking and for some stupid reason had hit me across the face. In response to that I shoved her back only to be screamed at and be told I was nobody and would always be nobody. I just walked out the front door after that and decided to walk off my fury even if it was like I was a volcano ready to erupt. I looked up and saw that Seth and Brad were already outside hanging out with a kid I had only seen once or twice before. I knew the kid they were talking to though. His name was Andrew Staboni. He was a short kid and about two years older than I was. He was in Brad's grade. He had to be five four at the most I'm guessing. He had blonde hair and was pretty well built for his size. He had that heavy Italian accent. You could see him playing a part in the Sopranos or something. He had the attitude to match the accent as well.

Andrew was pretty well known around the town. He usually had a short temper, which matched his height we would sometimes joke. I remember hearing about him getting angry with a clown because the clown patted him on the head. Andrew apparently turned to the clown as he was walking away and began yelling across the fair profane words at him. Later as the day went on Andrew saw the clown walking a little ways ahead of him. Andrew quickly grabbed one of the baseballs at one of the booths and threw it right at the back of the clown. The clown turned and the ball hit the clown right in the face, which was soon covered in blood. Andrew then yelled at the clown and told him where he could shove it. Ever since Andrew had been banned from the fair whenever it came into town. Andrew still has the baseball mounted on his wall, in what can only be described as some sort of trophy to him.

I walked over to them and was greeted. We started talking and I told them the event that had just taken place between my mom and me.

Seth then turned to me and said, "You want to go for a walk with us through the woods?"

At first I thought it was a pretty odd question, but I didn't think anything of it. "Sure why not," I replied, though, something in me gave me this queer feeling.

We began our walk through the woods. The sun hung high above the trees. The birds were chirping and it seemed like everything was alive. It was like a scene from one of those wild life shows. Everything was so beautiful that it almost seemed unreal to me. I almost thought I was dreaming. We walked deeper and deeper into the woods. I didn't think anything of it, well that was until we stopped.

I looked around the area. It was pretty well isolated from anybody's house. I could see the sun setting and just stared at it. I had no idea what my friends were planning to do, but it didn't really matter to me at that moment. All that mattered was watching the gleam of the sun over the treetops. I just stood there, a bit dumbfounded. Finally I shook all of my thoughts out of my head and turned to my friends. They were huddled in a group. What were they doing I thought as I looked at them? I would soon get the answer.

As I started walking towards them they turned to me. I finally saw what they were doing. I had never seen one before, but I had heard of it. It was a type cigarette but it wasn't. It was called a joint. I looked at them in confusion.

"So Jak," Andrew began, "you want to join us?"

A million thoughts began racing through my head all at once. What are they doing with pot? Why did they want me to have some? Why was I here? What would happen if I did? I had always been the good kid who stayed away from stuff like that. Suddenly I new thought began to enter my mind. I had always been the good one and I had gotten nothing for it. I was just another nobody without a real family. I was a loser with no future. I thought all of these things, and you know what, I was sick of it all. I was sick of being the good kid. It was all just one big joke.

As Andrew stretched his hand out to me, with the joint in it, I looked at my friends. I said to myself, this is my family.

I nodded my head and said, "You know what, why the hell not."

I took the joint and I began to smoke. It was like entering a confusing world of mystery and fantasy. Nothing made all that much sense anymore. I began to laugh with my friends at the stupidest stuff that we wouldn't have probably laughed about if we weren't stoned. I suddenly didn't feel so alone anymore. I didn't care about anything in the world. We smoked another joint after that. When we finished we all slowly got to our feet laughing because Brad had burned himself with the lighter. It was one of the oddest feelings yet funniest feelings I had ever felt.

We all headed back to our houses through the path in the woods that we had come. It was a lot darker as we headed back. I knew it was already nighttime, but some how it felt much darker than it was suppose to be. I didn't matter though. In fact I didn't care about anything at all. For the fist time I felt like I was my own person finally. Nothing in the world mattered to me anymore. I was Jak, I had to follow nothing and no one. I quietly made my way up the steps into the house. My mom was passed out on the couch with a bottle of Jack Daniels sitting on the table. I pulled the cover that was on the floor next to the couch over her. I then turned and made my way slowly up the stairs into my room watching my feet closely as I walked. When I finally made it I turned on my radio as I laid in my bed.

I began thinking the rules meant nothing now, nothing at all. There was no point in following them. Isn't that every kid's dream? No rules meant there isn't a thing bad you can do. You can do what ever you want and nothing and no one can stop you because you are free from the straps that've held you back. It's a party that will never end right? That's the draw back I realized. You see what kids don't realize is that sooner or later that party is just going to get out of control and some how someone is going to get hurt. Everything is going to change, even things you may not want to change. It's like driving a car with no brakes. If it keeps going on eventually you are going to want it to stop. The thing is you can't stop. You keep going until you crashed. There's a reason for rules, but we just choose not to see those reason. All we see are all of the drawbacks from these rules. We think about what we could do if those rules weren't there. It may look great, but there is just so much more to it. I didn't quite realize that until I had already crashed. By then it was too late.

I can't really explain all that had happened to me while I was in my room that night, but the next thing I knew I suddenly started to cry while I was laying in my bed. There was no real reason for it at all, I just did. I felt like I was inside the music in a sense. It was like every beat of the songs was some types of event in my life and they were flashing into my mind like lightning. The next thing I knew I was in some kind of dark room. It was so dark that I couldn't even see my hands in front of my face. It was a darkness unheard of. I got this peculiar feeling I wasn't alone in the room though. I looked down. I was watching someone from above. Upon looking at this person I came to the realization that the person I was watching was in fact myself.

I watched as I sat in a chair. Just sitting there, staring into the darkness. What was this I began to question? I watched myself stand up and feel my way through the darkness. Suddenly I was the one feeling my way through the darkness. It was so dark. It was almost scary in a way. Suddenly I felt myself begin to fall. I most have stepped into a hole because I was falling deeper and deeper into the darkness. What was this darkness that I was falling into? Why was it so cold? It was getting colder and colder the longer I fell into the darkness. A thought came to my mind. I than began to think that maybe this darkness was more than just darkness? Maybe, this darkness was in fact, my life and where it was going?

I suddenly woke up, sweating and breathing hard. It was almost like someone had just screamed in my ear. I was still in my room. I must have passed out during the night. My radio was still on so I turned it off, shook the cobwebs out of my head and headed downstairs. My mom had gotten up already and had left for work. She didn't make anything for breakfast, but it was okay. I made myself breakfast and thought nothing of the day before. It was nothing to me. Soon I would begin to smoke and drink with out any concern. With my mom always working it became easy for me to do it. It was almost like breathing for me I guess. It was just that easy to do. I was free to do what ever I wanted, and I was doing just that.

Even to this very day I still don't believe that it damaged my life in anyway. As much as the grown ups of my time would have said it would destroyed my life it wasn't what destroyed it, it was me. I was depressed yes, but I was already depressed. In fact all the trials it brought into my life actually helped me grow and mature as a person and a man. Not only that, but it made me come face to face with some of those inner demons I had tried to keep hidden with in me just like many others I knew. After I did it, it actually helped me realize a lot of the bad things I had going on for me in my life and that I had to change those things if I was to improve. I saw it destroy many of the people around me.

That didn't happen until I was in high school; that's really when things got interesting for me. That's when everything changed. Those were the years that made me the man I am today and though it may not seem like much, there's more to the picture than meets the eyes. It was like nothing I had ever gone through before. It was the changing point not only for me, but also from my point of view, for everyone. Sometimes though, in some ways, I kind of in a way wished that I hadn't gone through it. I had to though, and I guess it was worth it in the long run.

CHAPTER 3

PEOPLE OF THE SCHOOL

People Hiding

So many of us hide behind others
Disappearing and staying out of sight
No one knows, not even our own mothers
We keep trying to change with all our might

All thinking there is nothing wrong with us
Is it all true, or are we just lying
We have all been losing our faith and trust
When deep inside we are actually dying

The pain we feel from within is unreal
But we hide this pain by faking a smile
Not one person can tell us how it all feels
For they must first walk in our shoe for a mile

Then you will know how we are all feeling
For we are just the people who are hiding

Remember our names is all I ask from you this day
Because we are the ones hiding from all of our dismay

I wish to discuss the events of my high school years. Many things happened there. My first love and loss happened in high school. My growth from a boy to a man also happened there. I was like everyone in the sense that high school was the turning point in my life but in my case, it was a loop that I really wasn't prepared to deal with. I don't think many people are and if they say they are, they are most likely lying. It's something that I don't think any one can really be ready for.

I guess the best place to start is, well, my first day of high school. I walked in with Ron and it was like walking into a place where everything, the rules and people, had completely changed. Everyone had his or her own group to hang out with. I don't know why, but this bothered me. Maybe it was because there were so many groups or maybe it was just because I didn't fit into any of the groups. All I knew was that everything was going to be different.

I think these were the years I realized that people change. It's not that they want to, but more that they feel that they have to. As humans we feel that we have to fit into something, some group. It's funny in a way to me personally. People will promise their friends that they will always be there for them, but the second they get the chance to raise their popularity they forget that. Has that ever happen to you? The world's ways consume them and they are just like everyone else. Why do we do that? Why do we all need to have that feeling that we fit in? It's like a high that people are addicted to. I never really understood it until I entered high school. That's where you can see the change really take shape. No one really sees it unfortunately. They just say that people grow and change.

I was an average student I guess you could say. I did my work and kept to myself. No one would have guessed that I did all the things I did out of school. Pot became a daily thing for me after school. Drinking and partying became my weekend extravaganza. I made myself believe everything was great but yet, some where deep inside I had this feeling. I don't believe it was really a big feeling but it was enough that it always lingered in my mind. It was a feeling of loneliness. It was a loneliness that I wished to escape from.

I guess that is common at that age. It seemed to me that more and more kids during that time were coming out saying they felt depressed. Depression was in my view becoming far too common among teens. The question was why? No one really knows, but I had my thoughts. Even though I may have been one of those youth I always had my mind working. I believed that the reason kids feel depressed is that over the time growing up they lose themselves. They become these shells. I guess that is the best way to describe it. These shells get filled with this information from family, friends and anyone else in contact with the kid telling them what they should be. I don't think it's wrong, I mean that is the way things have always been. For some reason, though, it's becoming more effective now.

I see plenty of people I had once known change. They were these smart, innocent kids who were friendly to everyone. As we got older though and we finally reach high school I saw that change. It's like when you really believe you know someone and then they don't even realize that you are alive when you wave to them. The person changes so much that you really don't know them anymore. I promised myself that that would never happen to me. It would be a while though until I realized that I was indeed just like everyone else. I had changed but I had no idea that I had changed. I guess that is what happens to kids, as they get older. They don't realize the changes they are going through until one day they look at themselves and they are wondering who that is looking back at them in the mirror. I didn't at least until the changes took over my life. It was almost like I was trapped in a bubble that I had formed and there was no getting out of it, or was there?

I wouldn't find that out for a while. I went through high school not really paying attention. High school was a joke to me. I figured it was just a place where they tried to set us up for life and our future. I didn't see the point nor did I care. I just did the work to stay out of trouble. I guess I was still a good kid at heart despite how much I tried to change. That happens sometimes, right?

I think the only class I enjoyed was science. It wasn't because of the experiments or the fact that I got to cut things up, even though that was actually quite entertaining to me. No, it was more that I had some pretty cool teachers for my science classes. They really didn't bother me all that much which was always a plus in my book. I guess because I was a quiet kid. I just sat at my desk and did my work. They made things fun and interesting for me and I have to say those were some of the times I was actually happy in school.

To say I had a lot of friends in high school would be like telling you that the cat in the hat was really a giant dog. It just wouldn't fit with the actual truth. Due to my quietness not many people liked me or bothered to really get to know me. I guess I wasn't important enough to get to know. Amazingly, though, I liked it that way. I was like a rock and I figured making a lot of friends would just wear me away and soon I'd be nothing and blow away. That was probably a bad choice of thought when I think about it now because maybe I could have used the friends. I let my thick headedness take over me and it stopped me from making friends, and improving my life.

School had a wide range of people. Each person had their own personality some though stood out to me more than others did. I remember there were these two sisters. Their names were Melanie and Stephanie. Melanie was a short little red head girl. She would sometimes put on these weird contacts making her eyes look, well, trippy. Stephanie was a tall blonde girl. They both dressed in the skater girl fashion as people use to say. They also both usually had smiles on their faces. You really didn't see them frowning all that much.

If there were two people any crazier in the world than Melanie and Stephanie I would have been deeply afraid. The two of them were like the best of friends even though they were sisters. They just fit so well together. So well in fact that it would be scary to see what would have happened if they were separated from each other. I didn't think one would really be the same without the other from the way that they acted. It just didn't work that way. They always seemed to be so happy. They'd blurt things out of nowhere sometimes. It was enough for someone to think they suffered from turrets or something. Yet if you caught one of them alone and I mean alone, as in one of them was away from a group of people, you could really get into their heads. Stephanie interested me the most out of the two of them though. That was because she seemed more open to talk.

I remember it was at a party where we talked and I saw a different side of Stephanie. There was a lot of drinking going on at the party as usual. The kid having the party was home alone because his parents were out of town. So he decided to throw a "little" get together there. It was I'm guessing about 2:00 am Saturday morning. I'm not completely sure though because I was a bit tipsy myself. Most of the people though were asleep, or should I say passed out on the floor. That was how most parties I went to usually ended. Stephanie was still awake. She was sitting on the couch and I sat next to her and we just started talking. I think it was easier to talk openly because of us being drunk. We both didn't care though and we just kept talking. Then she really started to open up which kind of threw me for a loop. Now see what you need to know about Stephanie is that she was always trying to get a boyfriend. She'd go out with someone and they'd brake up and she'd need to get another one.

She looked at me and said, "You know what?"

"What?" I replied

"I think I know why I always want to have a boyfriend," She answered.

I looked at her and said, "And why is that?"

She took another sip of her beer and said, "I don't want to be alone. I need someone by me all the time, but something bad always happens when I get that person." I looked at her kind of oddly.

"I know," she said lowering her head, "you think I'm crazy."

"No, I think you are drunk," I replied with a smile. "Tell me though, why does something bad always happen?"

"Something bad always happens because I feel that the guy is trying to change me, but I don't want to change. Yet I get into a relationship hoping I can change that person," she said. "I guess it really doesn't work out that way. It's kind of contradicting."

"It is I guess," I replied, "but I can see what you mean."

She smiled at me and got up and made her way to the bathroom. I'm guessing she had a little too much to drink, but I still smiled. I had no idea Stephanie would be like that. She might have been drunk, but I think that is why I thought that was the real Stephanie and not the one everyone else saw. She didn't feel like she had to hide herself like everyone in the world does. No smiling when she felt like crying. No laughing when she wanted to scream. She was herself and she was proud of it. To bad it usually takes alcohol or something else to make people drop their guard and not care about the world around them. Isn't it? Why shouldn't we hide from the things we don't like about ourselves? It's safer that way right? I don't think it is. I think it just destroys us and yet, we really don't care if it does cause we put it into our minds we are okay. All these thoughts just don't compute in our minds.

Another person I met in high school was a local kid in my neighborhood. His name was Isaac. He was what many would call a straight arrow. For some reason we became pretty good friends even though we were complete opposites. I guess he was one of those positive things in my life. The kid loved music. I mean the only person I knew who loved music almost as much as Issaac was Ron. They'd always get together and talk about starting a band. It never happened though. I don't know why either. Isaac was a pretty cool kid. I had a lot of fun hanging out with him. Yet I don't think we were really that close. We'd say we were best friends, but as the years went on the more and more I realized we were growing farther apart. It came to the point that I really didn't know Isaac anymore, and he didn't know me. We were in two different worlds.

It always sucks when a friendship kind of disappears because people grow apart. I d didn't like it, but I realized a bit too late. I remember Isaac and me were talking one day about what we were going to do when we graduated.

"I'd like to be a cook," Isaac said, "and maybe play at some Jazz clubs on the side. What about you Jak?"

"Me," I exclaimed

"No, your cat stupid," Isaac laughed. "Seriously what do you want to do when you get out of school?"

I looked at Isaac and shrugged my shoulders. "I really don't know," I answered. I never really thought my life when I actually grew up.

That question actually made me think. I suddenly really started to think about my future. Isaac's question interested me. No one had really cared to ask me about my future. "Actually," I said, "I think I'd like to be a writer."

"Why is that," Isaac asked.

"Well," I started, "When I write I feel like for once, I can be myself. All my thoughts and ideas I can just put on a piece of paper and see for myself what is going on in my head. Not only that but also when I write and others see that writing and when they have an emotion I feel as if I've touched someone in some way. Even if they hate the writing I brought out some type of emotion. It's like you can connect to people on a totally different level."

Isaac nodded his head and responded by saying, "that's cool dude. I hope that works out for you."

That was one of the best conversations I had ever had with someone. What amazed me about it was that for once I opened up and I wasn't even high or drunk. I never did that before that day.

Another interesting character in school was the local pompous jock. I'm guessing every school has someone like that. The captain of some sports team who does what ever he wants and thinks he's the next biggest thing since plasma TV. In my case this person came in the form of Jason King. Jason was, no surprise, the captain of our school's football team. He was the quarterback, and I must admit that he was a pretty good one at that. He had to be at least six feet tall and compared to my height of five nine he pretty much loved shoving me and anyone else smaller than him around. He had this semi long brown hair that even after wearing a helmet during a game always seemed to be completely perfected, which made me sick. He had the jock body of muscles and ah yeah, more muscles. He wasn't the Incredible Hulk, but he was in pretty good shape. I wouldn't have minded being in as good of shape as he was.

Jason and I had bumped heads a couple of times during school, but we usually just avoided each other. He was in the popular crowd and I was in the loner group. Sometimes, though, you just can't avoid a conflict, especially when you are drunk and at a party. I was in my junior year of high school and my friends decided to throw a party. As the party went on Jason showed up with a couple of his football friends. They all started to drink with us and I really didn't think anything of it. Then things got a little bit crazy. Jason and his friends began trashing the place. I had had enough and got right in Jason's face.

"I think you've been here long enough," I said to him staring him eye to eye.

Jason looked down at me and laughed. "What the hell are you talking about," he laughed.

"Just go," I snapped. "You're trashing the place."

Jason smiled and it wasn't like just any smile. It was one of those yeah, right smiles, almost mocking me in a way.

"Look buddy," he snickered pushing me back, "we aren't going anywhere."

"Yes you are," I said.

I could tell I had struck a nerve in him. Jason turned to me and in a confused voice said, "What did you just say?"

The air suddenly took a deep change. Everyone at the party was quiet and looking at Jason and me. No one had ever stood up to Jason before.

"I said leave," I exclaimed.

I almost didn't believe the words coming out of my mouth. Actually I didn't believe I was actually speaking.

Jason got right in my face and yelled, "Do you know who the hell you are talking to shit head. No one tells me what to do."

He grabbed my shirt and pushed me to the ground. Something snapped in me as I hit the floor. I quickly got up as Jason was walking away. I grabbed his shoulder and spun him around. Like a bullet I swung and nailed him across the face. Jason stumbled back. His nose was bleeding. He touched the blood and glared at me with rage in his eyes. He let out a yell of anger and charged at me. Before I knew what was happening my feet were lifted up off the ground. I turned my head to see that we were heading towards a window. As if an explosion had gone off we crashed through that window unto the porch. Everyone at the party hurried outside to watch the fight. The only thing going through my head was "*I thought he was a quarterback, not a fullback?*"

The people at the party didn't get the chance to see a fight though. As they all headed outside flashing lights came on from the road. Apparently a neighbor had called the cops on the party. Since everyone was underage and had been drinking the entire party took off in every direction. Jason got off me and ran towards the woods. I got to my feet and headed that way to. Flashlights were all over the place trying to catch people from the party. I was glad that my friends and I had explored the woods a lot because even in the dark I could tell where I was heading. I found my way to a hole and hid in it. I don't remember what happened after that, but all I know is that some how I feel asleep in that hole.

I woke up the next morning hung over and really hungry. I made my way out of the woods and called Brad to see if he could pick me up. After he picked me up we headed to Burger King and had ourselves something to eat. The night before had definitely left its toll on me though. I found out that Jason got away, too, which kind of saddened me. I was hoping he got caught.

Now if Jason was the person in school I hated the most there was no one I loved more than Sarah Holland. Sarah was pretty much the same height as me so we would always look eye to eye. Her blue eyes were like a beautiful blue sky. If you looked into them long enough you would surely loose yourself in them. Her hair though was the thing that most people noticed about her. It wasn't really curly as it was frizzy, but it worked for her. She'd sometimes put it in a ponytail, but I liked it when she kept it untied. Those long curly hairs would just hang down and you would just feel this temptation to touch them. She seemed to always be smiling and up beat. Have you ever known someone that even on your worst day you just couldn't help but be happy when you saw them or they were around? That's how it was when I was around Sarah or saw her. I couldn't help but just smile when she smiled at me, and I couldn't help but be sad when she was sad. It's kind of hard to explain, but I felt in a way I was connected to her in some way.

I met Sarah in sixth grade, but we really didn't talk too much. We only talked in chess club. Ha, chess club. I still can't believe I actually joined that club back then. People, including you probably, always pictured chess club as this hangout for all of the smart kids with their pocket protectors and glasses. Yet it wasn't like that at all. Actually there were a lot of average kids there. I remember Sarah would always play against me. She had this goal that she was going to beat me, but she never did. She even went as far as to getting one of the smartest kids in our grade to help her try and beat me. I don't know how I did it, but some how I still beat her. I was Rocky and I had just knocked her out for the win. Though, I would have never hit Sarah. It was just our little thing that we did back then. After sixth grade, though, we kind of grew apart and didn't really talk all that much.

Then high school started. I had a couple of classes with Sarah and we started talking a lot more. Through our time together in high school we got pretty close. We'd always talk on line to each other. I began to realize that behind that shining smile of Sarah there was this sad little girl trying to escape from her cruel reality. I thought there was no one in the world more depressed than I was. Yet in some way I believed Sarah was more depressed than I was. We both hid it but I think I could deal with it a lot better than she could. She would tell me of times she would cry at night, afraid and alone. Her parents were separated like mine but there were a lot more problems in Sarah's. From what she told me the reason she did a lot of the things she did was because her parents didn't care what she did. They didn't care about her in any way she believed. It must be hard thinking your parents don't care about you. I wanted to say something to comfort her but I couldn't for some reason. I couldn't relate to what she was going through but I wish I did. I wanted to help her in anyway possible. She would say everything was okay, but from looking at the cuts on her wrist I knew everything wasn't. Still, though, I couldn't say anything to comfort her. It was like she was drowning in an ocean of pain and all I wanted to do was jump into the water and save her, but I couldn't because I couldn't swim. I would just stand there watching her hurt herself. If anything, that's what hurt me the most.

Sarah had an interesting best friend. Her name was Jessica Murry. She was about five, five in high school I'm guessing. She had this long dirty blonde hair and wore glasses most of the time. There are few people that interest me more than Jessica. It wasn't because I wanted from her what most guys at the time wanted from her. No, I wasn't one of her many shadows that followed her around. That just wasn't me. You see the reason she interested me was because of her whole personality. When you first meet Jess she seems like this shy girl. You can try and start a conversation with her but it usually doesn't go all that far and you end up feeling like a complete looser. At least that's how I felt the first time I talked her. It just seemed like she just didn't want to talk to me so I really didn't bother.

That seemed to be so far in the past later on. In the future we'd talk and I'll actually see a smile on her face. You see, though, I still wasn't complete sure of everything. Even now I wonder if maybe there was still so much more about her that I didn't know. You know how some people laugh and you wonder if they are actually laughing because what was said was funny or just because they felt that they had to. That always went through my head when I saw her smile or laugh. I'd talk to her friends and hear all these great and interesting things about her yet I never saw it. I wanted to, but I figured there was no point. I remember talking to Sarah one day about something and in that conversation we got to talking about Jessica. Sarah just went on and on about how much Jessica meant to her.

Somewhere in all of this I said to her, "That Jess seems great, I wish I knew her."

Sarah replied to that and said, "Yeah, when you really get to know Jess though she's amazing. I don't think I could ever live if anything bad happened to her."

I thought of all the times I had seen something bad happen to Sarah and how Jess seemed to always be that stone for Sarah to hold onto as a river of pain just pushed on her trying to drag her away. Jess seemed so strong and it seemed almost like she could deal with just about anything that the world through at her. Yet sometimes when something bad happened I think she just held in the pain she really felt inside herself. You could see it in her eyes though. She'd always kind of have this out of it look to her. Like a lost child in a library you could say, but when you looked into her eyes you knew there was so much more. There was something hidden beneath the surface you saw.

I'm usually good at breaking people down and knowing the person inside that they try to hide. I'd do everything I could to figure them out. It usually worked out pretty well but it really wasn't working on Jess. I'm guessing that all the people I had gotten to open up before just weren't strong enough mentally to hold it all in. Jess was tough I was guessing. I based a theory on what I had heard Jess was like from those closest to her and how I saw her. That theory was that she wasn't that much different from me in the sense that she only let certain people really get to know her. I was basing this all on what I thought though. The fact is, yeah I didn't know her. I was going to try and get her to open up to me when she felt like she wanted to. It never really happened though but for some reason I was okay with that. Sometimes you just can't get to know everyone in the world. If only seeing her smile, laugh or say something funny was all I'd know about her, well, then it was a lot better than not knowing her at all.

There were so many different personalities when I was in school. In any school you go to you can see a diverse group of people that are so different that you sometimes wonder how they all can be in one place. You would figure there would be just this explosion waiting to happen because you couldn't see how all these people could be together and yet be so different. If you thought that then maybe you haven't looked outside your window lately. Here in the United States we live in a world of cultural diversity you can say. So many different nationalities live in this country. You can say, "Oh but this is a big country," but that would only be partly true. I mean, with all the people here it doesn't seem as big as it actually is. The fact is that more than three fourths of those people have different nationalities. So it's actually no different from the world, just smaller.

Everyone in school had their own personality and groups. That's what separated everyone, groups. Even if you wanted to be in high school or not you were classed into a group. It was like we were in a classed society in school. Almost like how it use to be in India. If you look back to when you were in high school I bet you can see how I can say that and if you are a high school student now you are seeing it probably everyday. You hang out with the so-called "homies" you are judged by that. If you want good grades, or you are snobby than you're a "Prep." If you listen to heavy metal you're a "Metal head". If you skate you're a "Skater." The list goes on and on with groups people can be placed into. The group you may be placed into may fit you or it may not. No one cares though which group you wanted to be a part of. It just didn't work that way.

I guess the group I was closest to would be the "outcast" group. That was a group basically created for those that didn't really fit into a group. This group was different from the others in the sense that no one in the group was very similar. Everyone did their own thing and didn't care what others thought. Amazingly I actually enjoyed being in this group. You weren't the most popular person, but I liked that. The less popular you are the smaller the amount of people who would talk to you. I was pretty much left alone during school, which was quite nice for me.

Chapter 4

Lost So Much

The Pain

A suffering so surreal
All of it I don't think I can deal

Why did I have to loose so much
All for just one single touch

I've lost my love, my friend's, my life
And now I'm only left with this knife

What did I do
That some how I hurt you

Everyone has left me alone
And I can only cry and moan

I feel so sad
Yet I'm so mad

All I wanted was fame
Now I'm only left with this pain

When you loose someone have you ever wondered why you had to loose them? Like why them and not you? That question has been a part of my life for what seems like forever. It just seems to stick with me like a bad itch. I try and pretend it's not there, but I know it's there and at some point I'm going to scratch it. I just wished that there were another option.

Why do I wonder this you are probably asking yourself? Well the thing is I have lost a lot in my life. I mean I have lost things that I would never pray or wish for anyone else to loose. Actually I should say people. Yes, people. It seemed almost like all the people who got close to me, or I got close to, seemed to one day just disappear forever. Who exactly? Well I'll tell you but first just think of everyone you have met so far. You done? Now think about how you would feel if they were gone. Okay, now I guess we can begin.

The first person I lost was none other than my dad. I still remember the day I found out. It was August 15, 2003 and I was hanging out with Seth and Brad. My mom was out of town. She was giving herself a little vacation, which I thought she deserved. That left me with the house all to myself. I took full advantage of it just like any normal teenager. I had friends over nearly every night. I'd hang out all night and sleep all day unless I had to go to work. Since I had my license and a car I'd go out partying with my friends all week long as well.

I was heading out of my house I remember. Seth, Brad and me where heading up to a party. The phone rang, though, before I could reach the door. I was arguing with myself over if I should answer it or not. I decided to answer it just in case it was my mom. When I answered it a strange voice was on the line. It wasn't someone that I recognized, but they were asking for my mom.

"My mom isn't here," I answered, "who is calling may I ask?"

"This is the hospital down in Greenville, Maine. We are calling regarding a Mr. James Davis."

"That's my dad," I exclaimed. "What is a matter with my dad? Is he okay? What's wrong?"

There was a moment of silence. My heart was beating faster and faster as the seconds passed by in silence. Finally a voice responded to me. The phone slipped out of my hands and I dropped to my knees. Apparently my dad had fainted in a parking lot. He had had a heart attack. It was pretty bad and the doctors were amazed that he lived for as long as he did. It was for no good though. When he had fainted a car was coming by and hit him. His spine had been fracture and he had extreme head trauma. He was in a coma and died shortly after arriving at the hospital. The doctor told me it was a peaceful death. This angered me in how he could say that. What the hell did it matter if he suffered? He was dead. I was never going to see him again. Yet the doctor thought it would all be better some how by telling me he didn't suffer when all I wanted was my dad back.

I hung up the phone and then called Seth and Brad. I told them to go on without me. After I got off the phone I went up to my room and just sat there in the dark. My world was spinning around. I just sat and cried. It was like someone was just ripping every single strand of hair out of my head one by one. I was hurting and there was nothing I could do. When my mom got home I gave her the biggest hug I had ever given anyone. She was all I had left now and I didn't want to loose her. I told her what happened and she tried to comfort me like any good parent would. It just didn't help though. We couldn't go to the funeral since we couldn't afford to go up there. My mom and I both needed to work to pay off bills.

Life just seemed to suck so much. I tried to think positive though. You know, think like hey it couldn't get worse. Ha, and just like that things just seemed to get worse and worse. I was doing badly in school, kids seemed to just enjoy picking on me anymore and my mom was coming home drunker and drunker every night. Why is it that when you think it couldn't get worse it does? It just isn't fair. The fact is that it's bullshit and nothing else. What is the point for us to hate living? What just because everything is going bad for us? We can grow from it yeah, but it sure is hard to do when you just begin hating life. Maybe it was just me, though, but nothing seemed to be working out and it would only get worse later on.

I believe the only good thing going for me at the time was Sarah. Since I could drive I could see her more often, which is exactly what I did. We just seemed to, connect in a special way. You know it's kind of like when you meet that special person or persons and you just seem to click. You can talk to that person about anything and they can talk to you about anything. It doesn't matter what. That's how it was with Sarah. She could tell me anything that was on her mind and I could tell her anything that was going through my mind.

I don't know, maybe it was love. Though if you asked me back then I would have denied it. I don't know though. I just felt something when I was around her. I could be myself and still be happy when I was with her, which was a pretty big thing for me. I don't know that she felt the same way but it didn't matter I guess. As long as she was there I was happy. I could be in the worst mood and just seeing her would cheer me up right away.

The only bad thing that came from me hanging out with Sarah so much was that it put a strain on my friendship with Seth. Seth had his own girlfriends, but it was usually one of those "beneficial" relationships if you get what I mean. The two of us would still hang out a lot though. Yet soon I found myself hanging out more and more with Sarah. That meant that less and less of the time I spent with Seth. Why is it that usually people are left with the choice of either their friends or the ones that they love? You have to choose one but to do that you have to loose and hurt the other. The thing is you don't want to loose one or the other and you are left confused. Sometimes it can all work out but sometimes it just doesn't. For me, that's exactly what happened. I hurt one of the ones I cared about and couldn't say I was sorry.

It was late one night at this kid Alex Baker's house when something I would never forget happened. Alex was throwing a party and pretty much everyone from school was going. He basically lived in a giant house. It had three floors not including the basement and attic. His parents were pretty rich so he had a giant plasma TV and one of the biggest sound systems you've ever seen. His basement had a home made bar in it and since Alex's parents went to Hawaii for their anniversary the bar would come into a lot of use. So Seth, Ron, Brad and me decided we would head over to the party. Brad and Seth went in Brad's car and Ron and I went in my car. We arrived at the party around 10:45 P.M. A couple of people were already there, but most of the people arrived at 12:00. There was drinking, smoking, sex and everything that made a party a party back in my day. Something was wrong though. I can't really explain it, but I had this bad feeling. It was like a pinch on the back of neck. I washed away those fears, though, with a couple more beers.

The party went on and on. With every hour everybody got more and more trashed. Soon it was like we were all in a blender and everything was spinning. I began making my way outside. I guess all the spinning was finally getting to me. I made it outside and found Seth sitting on the step.

I sat next to him. “What’s up dude,” I said in a kind of slurred speech.

“Nothing,” he replied in a kind of snappy tone. He was drunk too but something was bothering him and I didn’t know what.

“What’s wrong man, seriously?” I asked.

“None of your business,” Seth snapped back at me.

He got to his feet and started to walk away.

“What the hell is your problem?” I yelled.

“My problem,” Seth exclaimed, “don’t give me that what’s your problem bull shit. You know damn well what it is.”

“What the hell did I do?” I questioned

“What did you do? What the hell do you think you did? You just go ad ditch me for some bitch so can get some ass and you ask me what you did. You betrayed our friendship dude. All you care about anymore is her, I mean we use to hang out all the time. Now look, we barely see each other anymore, let alone know each other. What makes it even worse is that you don’t even seem to give a rat’s ass about it,” Seth yelled. “You just care about yourself now!”

“First off,” I started as I got to my feet, “It’s nothing like that. Yeah I hang out with Sarah, but I still hang out with you.”

“Rrrrrrrrrrrrright,” Seth laughed, “if that’s so true then when was the last time we hung out together before tonight?”

I paused.

"Exactly what I'm saying," he continued, "we barely know each other anymore. About the only time I see you is in school and that is hardly ever. You are too busy trying to get ass to even say hi to me anymore."

"It's nothing like that," I snapped back, "you know that.

"Oh is it?" Seth questioned. "Then what is, then?"

"I don't know," I answered

"Well then there's nothing for us to talk about," Seth declared. He turned and started walking. He then stopped, turned back and said, "You know what?"

"What," I asked.

"You were my first real friend," he said, "but now I don't even know."

Seth got in Brad's car and pulled away." I just stood there in disbelief. Had we really grown that far apart? Suddenly I was angry. I was angry with Seth, myself, and just about everything. I reached down and picked up a pile of stones and threw them at the car as it drove away.

"FUCK YOU," I yelled.

I fell to the ground and began to cry. What was happening to me I thought? I wiped my face and rejoined the party. I just sat through the rest of it. Finally early the next morning Brad, Ron, and I left. Since Ron hadn't really done much he drove us home. I just sat there in the passenger side of my car as we drove back looking out the window and thinking about my argument with Seth. Maybe he was right. Maybe I was kind of taking him for granted. As we pulled up to my house Ron parked my car in the front and we got out.

Ron and I headed into my house as Brad headed up to his house. I was fighting with myself about whether I should've gone with Brad to talk to Seth or not but ultimately I decided to just give him some space until the time was right. Ron and me entered my house and got ourselves something to eat. As we sat there eating I just couldn't get everything that happened the night before out of my head. Suddenly my thoughts were thrown to the side as a sudden pounding came from my back door. I got up and ran to the door. As I opened it Brad came running in.

"Brad," I questioned, "what are you doing over here?"

Brad struggled to catch his breath but finally he gasped, "You need to get me over to the hospital now."

"What's wrong," Ron asked.

"It's Seth," Brad stammered. "He got into an accident when he left the party. My mom left a note on the door saying that they were at the hospital and for me to get over there as quickly as possible. So you have to give me a ride, please?"

I just stood there. Frozen, frozen with fear. Was Seth going to be okay? What happened? Why am I just standing here? All these thoughts were going through my head at this time.

"Jak, you okay?" a voice asked.

I cleared my head and saw that it was Brad asking if I was all right. I nodded my head finally to signify that I was okay.

"Okay," Brad said. "Well can you give me a ride?"

"Yeah," I replied. "Let's go."

I grabbed my jacket and Ron, Brad and I filed out the door to my car. As we got in the car I pulled out my keys. My hand started shaking as I tried to put the key in the ignition. It was so bad in fact that I couldn't start the car.

"How about I drive," Ron suggested. I nodded my head and got out of the car and got in the passenger seat. Ron started the car and we headed to the hospital.

The car ride seemed to take forever. It felt like we were barely moving at all. When we arrived at the hospital I suddenly wished it had taken longer. Now don't get the wrong idea about me. I wanted to see Seth. Hell, he was my best friend. It was just that I kept on going back to the party and our argument. I mean the last thing I said directed to him was fuck you. I just couldn't forget that. It had happened and I couldn't just go back and change that even though it was all I wanted to do.

As we walked into the hospital my heart began to beat faster and faster. He has to be alive I told myself. He just had to be. I mean he was Seth. I kept thinking about all the times we hung out with each other. He and I laughing at something the other one did. Going for walks and just talking about everything that was going on. Chilling at parties and getting drunk or stoned. What if there weren't going to be anymore of those times? What if, just what if I was going to loose my best friend for good? How would I go on was all I was thinking. How would I?

You know it's funny if you think about it. You see, sometimes we neglect our friends, whether we think about it or not. Why do we do it though? Well the fact is we do it because we figure our friends are always going to be there no matter what. We never think about what would happen if they weren't there. That thought just doesn't process through our minds. Then one day it happens and they are gone and we are left in amazement. We never saw it coming, nor were we prepared for it either. Our friend is gone forever. Something we thought that not even God could end has finally ended. There is no more hanging out or seeing them. All that is left now is just another memory that we would cherish forever until the day we died.

Everything looked like it was in slow motion as we made our way up to Seth's room. It was like we were in some type of time warp. It felt as if I had a ton of bricks attached to each of my ankles. My feet just seemed to drag across the floor. I just wanted it to be over with. I wanted to see Seth and have it done with. I couldn't go on if I didn't see him for one more time.

Finally though, we made it to his room. His mom and dad were there with him. His mom had her head down on the bed. She was crying. Brad and Ron entered. I just stood there in the door way though. Seth's face was pretty bruised up and you could see the cuts on his face. It was one of the most disturbing things I had ever seen. If it wasn't for the monitor by his bed you could have sworn he was already dead.

Suddenly I couldn't hear anything but the beeping of the monitor. It was almost as if everything was covered in darkness and the only things that could be seen were Seth, his bed and me standing in the doorway. Everything else just didn't exist. Emotions just took over me. I was scared, sad, worried, and angry all at the same time. Any other emotion you could think of, I was going through.

Seth's mom looked up at me. Her eyes were red from crying so much. I'm glad you came," she said to me.

"I just couldn't sit at home," I replied. "He's my best friend."

As I talked to her I continued to just stare at Seth. He was and would always be my best friend. Why did this all have to happen? Why couldn't it have been me instead of him? I just wanted to run out of the room and keep running. Just run until I couldn't run anymore.

My heart wouldn't let me do that though. If I just left my best friend while he was lying in a hospital bed fighting to stay alive I wouldn't be able to live with myself. That's when you know someone means something to you. When you see them in trouble and you can't bear to leave them. It's like your life means nothing at the moment. All that matters is your friend. That's how I felt. Seth was my first real friend and now I was going to have to face the fact that he just might not be around for much longer. I kept thinking he couldn't die. Not now at least. We were going to go cross-country when he graduated.

How could I go now without him? If he was gone then who was left for me to talk to about the real me that no one else but him actually saw?

I turn to Seth's mom. "Do you mind if I could have a little time alone with him," I asked.

"I guess that could be done," Seth's mom answers. "I could use another box of tissues any way."

With that Seth's family and Ron left the room. That just left Seth and me. I pulled a chair over next to him and sat down. I just sat there staring at him.

"You really screwed up man," I finally said. "You just had to start with me. Why? Was it really that important?"

I just stared at him as tears rolled down my cheeks.

"What happened man? We use to never have any problems like this. Now look at us. We were almost at each others throats."

I got up and walked over to the window and stared out it. I turned back to Seth and said, "I know you probably can't hear me, but I'm sorry. You are my best friend. Hell you were my first real friend and you deserved better from me. The thing is that I get this strange feeling when I'm around Sarah. It's like I'm finally complete. It was a feeling a got addicted to but I didn't realize I was hurting you in the process."

I walked back to the bed and got on my knees beside him. "You just have to be okay," I whimpered as I started to cry. "I want you to know that you were one of the few people I trusted. You were always there for me and I failed you. When you needed me I just kind of pushed you to the side and I'm sorry for that. No one deserves that, especially you. Do you remember that time my mom kicked me out and you let me stay at your house for a while? I went up to go to sleep and you were nowhere to be seen. I didn't know where to sleep so I just kind of sat there in your room on a chair waiting for you. Then your mom came in and asked me where you were. I said I had no idea where you were. Then we looked to the floor between your bed and the wall and there you were sleeping on the floor. You decided to give up your bed for me to sleep in. You were and probably the only person who ever did something like that for me."

I wiped the tears off my face. Seth still wasn't moving, but I kept talking.

"You know what," I began, "I never told you this, but you were like my older brother. Yeah sure you're younger than I am and all, but it made no difference. I always looked up to you. So you can't go, you just can't. I need my big brother."

Suddenly the beeping on the monitor began to slow down.

"No, damn it," I yelled. "Don't you fucking give up! You can't go. Not now, please don't."

Slower and slower the beeping went until finally it stopped. I just stared at Seth. He was gone, gone forever. I fell to the floor and just sat there.

You know that feeling you get when you see a friend or someone you care about is crying? Well that's how I felt, only it felt ten times worse. I had just lost my best friend. You've probably heard it before, but truth be told, I honestly would have given anything for it to have been me instead of him or to just have one more day. There weren't going to be any more jokes or fun times. There weren't going to be any more times of walking around and just talking about each other's lives. No, that was just going to be a faded memory now. One I would always cherish. I got to my feet and went out and got Seth's parents. They both came rushing in and started crying. I walked out of the hospital and sat on the curb.

There's a time to cry and there's a time not to cry. Yes, my best friend was gone but this wasn't one of those times to cry. I had to be strong. Not just because Seth would have wanted it that way, but also because I had to be for myself. Ha, I could see Seth looking at me and seeing me cry. He'd probably make some crack at me like calling me a sissy or tell me to suck it up because real men don't cry. That wasn't going to happen though. I didn't want to cry any ways though because I didn't want my last memory of Seth to be a sad memory. I wanted to have my last memory of Seth to be something I could look back upon and smile about. Sometimes you just have to be strong to go through the pain that life throws at you and that's exactly what I was going to do.

I went to Seth's wake and funeral. While everyone around me was crying I still refused to cry even though it was tearing me up inside. When we finally made it to the cemetery Seth's mom asked me to speak. I was completely caught off guard but I sucked it up and did it anyway. I owed it to Seth. Standing there and looking around at Seth's entire family and friend though kind of freaked me out a little.

Finally I said, "Seth…Seth was my best friend. I can't remember a time when he was never there for me, and for anyone else who needed him. Some may say he didn't really do the best things with his life. That at times may have been true but I have to say that the good far outshines the bad. Seth never really asked much from anyone. The only thing he really ever asked for is for others trust and respect."

I paused to hold back from crying at that moment and in a sadden voice I said, "Seth was unlike any one I have ever met in my life. Just by the way he carried himself. I always thought he was invincible and that nothing could ever stop him. He may be gone but the fact is that he really isn't dead. The only way he could truly be gone is if all of us here today forget him. I hope and pray that never happens and I ask that no one here today lets that happen."

I turned to Seth's coffin and with the most confident voice I could muster up I said, "Thanks, Seth. Thanks for making my life mean just that much more."

I will always remember Seth. He taught me a lot about life. Sometimes things happen that you just can't control. Why you ask? Well think of it this way, if we could control everything that happened around us we could never truly grow. We'd still be at the same level for all of our lives. Some may think that that would be better, but I'd have to disagree. If we could stop hardships from happening the world would be perfect and as we all know, nothing is perfect. It's just how it all works out. We can get angry, but there's no point for it. If anger is all you feel when you experience loss then you are wasting energy that could be used for other things. Anger I believe is just an excuse to not face what is truly bothering you. You just have to realize that for yourself and out grow it.

To those people who have lost someone, I am sorry. It's not an easy process to deal with or get over. To you I say life can get better if you want it to be. Sometimes letting go, though it may seem hard, is the best thing you could do for yourself. When I say let go though I don't mean just forget about that person or people you've lost but rather I mean go on with life the best you can. Live life to the fullest but always keep a special place in your heart for that person or people you've lost. It's the only way you can go on with your life really.

Unfortunately for me things just didn't get easier. How is probably the question going through you're mind. Well I can't tell you right away but I'll lead up to it. You see there were a lot of things that added up to this moment. In fact this was probably the moment that changed my life forever. Not that loosing both Seth and my dad wasn't bad enough, but I mean this one just destroyed me. It's also the reason, in many ways, why my view on life completely changed.

To start off I guess I have to explain some of the events that lead up to my most painful moment. There was a party about a year and a couple of months after Seth's accident. I hadn't gone to any parties after that but Ron got me to go. He said it would be good for me. I kind of turned into a hermit you can say. The only time I went out was for three reasons. One, my mom needed help at the store. Two, it was nice out and I couldn't stand staying inside. The third reason was to hang out with Sarah. Other than that I usually stayed inside listened to music, working out or reading. Sarah got me into reading. Usually she would have me read poetry. I use to think poetry was some girly thing, but after a while I began to enjoy it.

Well anyway I decided to go to this party just for the heck of it. I thought hey who knows, I might even have fun. So I met up with Ron and Brad and we headed up to the party. Apparently it was going to be an early graduation party. Brad was already going to college, but he was on a break so that's why he was coming with us. The kid throwing the party had a beach house that his parents got for him. So he decided to have a beach party to celebrate the graduation.

When we got there it seemed as if everyone in school was there.

We saw a couple of people carrying in some kegs. Brad laughed and said, "Well guys if you need me you know where to find me."

With that Brad followed the kegs. Brad seemed okay with Seth's death, well on the outside. Besides Seth, Brad had two older brothers, two younger sisters about three and five years younger than Seth, and a little brother about four years old. The thing is Brad really didn't talk or hang out with the others. Seth and Brad were usually the ones that got along the best in the house. If there was a party being planned it was usually them planning it. So not only did Brad loose a brother, but he also lost a friend in a sense. If you talked to Brad about it, though, he wouldn't say it, but just by the look in his eyes with the mention of Seth's name you could tell there was a still a strong bond there. Brad would usually drink or smoke to hide it. It probably wasn't the best decision he made.

Ron looked around then turned to me. "You see, dude, this is going to be great," he declared.

"I guess," I replied, but I wasn't too sure.

We entered the party and began talking and drinking with people. I have to say I was enjoying myself. The party wasn't as bad as I thought it was going to be. A lot of the people I talked to in school were there and amazingly Jason King and I were actually talking instead of trying to rip each other's throats out. In fact, for the first time I actually felt as if I fit in.

As the night went on, and let me tell you it went on, I felt a tap on my shoulder. I turned around and saw Ron standing there. "What's up?" I asked.

"I think Sarah just got here with her boyfriend," Ron said.

"Okay," I replied. "Why are you telling me?"

"I really don't know," Ron laughed. Ron was pretty trashed. He was lucky his girlfriend Jody was there to hold him up. Those two were perfect together. They just fit so well together, despite their different personalities. I remember I asked Ron one day as to why he cared so much about Jody. To me it didn't make sense to be so young and in love.

Ron simple looked at me with a slight grin and said, "I don't know. All I can say is that when I'm with Jody I feel, no, I know I've found something special. I don't just hang out with her because she's my girlfriend. I hang out with her because I want to. I feel like when I'm with her I'm more then I use to be. I'm complete. Maybe it's love, maybe it's not. Personally, I could care less. All that matters is that I'm with her, and she's with me. That's all I could have ever asked for. It's when you find someone who makes you feel that way that you know you don't want to lose them."

I thought about that as they walked away and Jody puked on Ron's shoes. I decided after a laugh or two because of that I'd go around and talk to people. I may have been talking, but I kept thinking about Sarah. I knew she had a boyfriend, but I still liked her. I just wasn't going to do anything to break up her relationship with her boyfriend. The guy was an asshole in my personal view and that wasn't because he was with Sarah. He just didn't treat Sarah the way that she should have been treated. I didn't say anything though because Sarah liked him. So I wasn't going to do anything to destroy that for her.

It was close to 1:00 A.M. I believe when I began walking around the beach house. People seemed to be hooking up all around. It's amazing what happens when you gather a group of hormone driven teens into an area. It seems like anything goes and it doesn't matter whom or what sees them. I made my way outside where I saw that Brad's car was shaking. I was about to go and break it up, but I saw Ron's shoes hanging out the window. I decided Ronny boy was getting some and he wouldn't be too happy if I interrupted him, no matter how funny it would have been. So I decided to go and walk down to the beach instead. I thought maybe things would be a little calmer down there. Once again I would be proven wrong.

Walking down I got this strange feeling. It was almost like something was taking over me and telling me which way to go. I began hearing something. People were talking over the hill I was walking on. I peered over the hill and saw two people sitting on the beach. I was about to walk over to see who they were when I heard them talking.

Now don't think badly of me here okay. I'm not one to eavesdrop, but by the way they were talking it seemed as if they weren't in the best of moods. Heck, they sounded down right pissed. So I decided just to sit at the top of the hill and listen to them a little before I made my way down.

"Come on," the male voice said. "We can do it right here on the beach."

"I already said no," the female voice replied. "You're drunk any ways. You always do this. We go to a party, you get drunk and all you think about is sex."

"What the hell is up with you?" he questioned.

"Nothing," she answered.

"Don't give me that bullshit," he snapped. "You've been acting different now for a while. I'm your boyfriend and I deserve some answers."

"Maybe that's the problem," she snapped back.

"What," he asked.

"You're my boyfriend," she barked at him.

There was a moment of silence after that. It was like some sad soap opera.

Finally the girl broke the silence as she turned and said, "I think we're done."

She began to walk away from the boy and up the hill where I was hidden.

Suddenly there was a yell of anger and the boy was running up the hill after her.

"You stupid bitch," he screamed. "It just doesn't work like that."

He tackled her to the ground and slaps her. He then began trying to rip her clothes off. This was too much for me and I got up from my hiding place and ran down towards them. The boy didn't see me until

I had tackled him off the girl and was on top of him. I punched in the face a couple times then got off him.

"Get the hell out of here," I barked. He got up and ran off. My body was shaking a little. I turned and walked over to the girl. I saw something shiny lying on the ground next to her and picked it up. It was a necklace with the name Sarah on it. I froze and stared at the girl. It was too dark so I couldn't tell who it was.

"Sarah?" I asked.

The girl got up and looked at me.

"Jak," she exclaimed.

She jumped onto me and gave me a huge hug.

"I'm so happy to see you," she said in tears. "I don't know what would have happen if you didn't show up."

I don't know why, but I began to cry at this time as well.

"Are you okay?" I asked.

She nodded her head then tightened her grip around me. I walked her back up to the party. Sarah's boyfriend Frank had high tailed it out of there by the time we had reached the beach house. We just sat down on the steps of the beach house. Sarah was shaking and crying. I really didn't know what to do so I just put my arm around her and told her everything was going to be okay. Soon she stopped crying and we just sat there for the rest of the night. She called Jess to come pick her up around 4:15 am.

When Jess arrived Sarah and I stood up. I walked her toward Jess' car. She turned to me and looked me in the eye.

"Thank you," she said.

She still had tears in her eyes. A tear ran down her cheek. I reached out my hand and brushed the tear away. She stared at me. The next thing I knew, she kissed me. It wasn't one of those big dramatic kisses that you see in the movies. No it was a more of a peck on the lips, but that didn't really matter. Have you ever loved someone so much that just the simplest thing they did meant the world to you? Sarah turned and got in the car and they drove off. I felt almost like I was floating high in the clouds. I didn't even realize that they ran over my foot as they drove away. Ha, I just felt like I was on top of the world.

I went back inside and helped Ron carry Brad out. Since I wasn't that entirely drunk I was the one who had to drive. Driving back, though, I felt like I could crash at any moment. I was so happy that I really wasn't paying much attention to the road. We made it back home in one piece thankfully. I dropped Ron and Brad off and headed up to my house.

Walking in I saw my mom lying on the couch. She had once again been drinking. I was about to just go up to my room, but for some reason I stopped. I walked over to the couch and pulled a blanket over my mom. I gave her a kiss on the forehead and whispered, "I love you ma." I then turned and went up the stairs excited and over joyed about the events that just took place. For once things were actually looking up. That's something I never thought would have happened. I went to sleep with a smile on my face that night. It was smile so great that if it could glow, it'd shine so bright that all those who saw it would have been stricken blind.

The next event leading up to my big loss was my senior trip. It was decided that we were heading down to the sunny beaches of Florida. After some beach time we would head over to Disney World. To tell you the truth, it all sounded a little bit childish to me. I knew I wasn't a grown up yet, but still the thought of taking pictures with a giant mouse and duck didn't sound all that fun to me. Then again, if it didn't consist of a beer bong back then it really didn't sound all that appealing to me.

I went anyways, though. I can't really tell you why. It was just one of those things you do, no questions asked. The idea of spending the nights in a hotel with someone looking over my shoulder every minute wasn't exactly the ideal thing for me to deal with, but hey, with all the crap going on there had to be something good coming out of it I thought. The question was what was that good thing? Take a second or two to think. Well just listen on and you'll find out.

When we arrived in Florida our hotel was right by a Hooters bar. Sorry, though, that wasn't the good thing. You see that first night there we were allowed to walk around the area as long as we were back in our rooms before curfew. Of course everyone took full advantage of this freedom and hurried out. Well I shouldn't say everyone. There was one idiot who decided to stay back. Yes, that idiot was no other than little old me. Don't be too surprise now. You see I just didn't feel like walking around and joking with people. Like I've said, I wasn't exactly a *"people person"*. So instead of walking around to all of the shops I decided just to go out to the back of the hotel. I figured no one would be there so I could

The hotel we were staying at was right next to the ocean. So when you walked out you could see right across the big blue. Of course, with me, I had to be outside to see the sunset. It was like an addiction. I had accepted it. So there I sat in the grass watching the sun slowly set. The mixture of colors in the sky was amazing. My attention was soon drawn towards the finger tapping me on the shoulder. I turned and there smiling at me was Sarah.

I couldn't really tell which was more beautiful, the sunset or the beautiful girl smiling at me. Sarah sat down next to me.

"What are you doing?" she asked.

"Watching the sun set," I replied. "Aren't you going to go shopping like everyone else?"

"Do you not want me here?" she questioned.

"No," I exclaimed. "I was just wondering why you want to sit here with me instead of walking around with your friends."

"You are my friend," she said with a smile. At that moment it was pretty hard not to just smile and blush. I tried, to not much success, but I tried. Sarah smiled at me then gets a serious look on her face.

"What's up?" I asked.

"Nothing," she answered.

"Don't tell me that," I said. "Come on, tell me."

She turns to me and in the calmest voice she can make she said, "I never really thanked you for helping me at that party. I mean I don't know what would have happened if you weren't there."

"I was there," I said. "That's all that's matters. You don't have to thank me for anything."

"But I do," she declared. "You were there for me when I needed you. It wasn't by chance. Something just tells me you were there by more than coincidence."

I began thinking back to that night. Something did lead me over to Sarah and her boyfriend. What did that mean? I looked into Sarah's eyes and saw that tears were building up in her eyes. I reached my hand out and brushed her cheek. "Don't cry," I said. "You don't have to cry."

I then began feeling my own eyes begin to tear up. What was going on I asked myself.

Looking at Sarah I whispered, "No matter what, happens I will always be there for you."

"Thank you," she said as a tear rolled down her rosy checks. What happened next, I can't really explain. Sarah leaned over and hugged me. It felt like we were locked up in this hug for what seemed like eternity. Then when it finally ended, I kissed her. I don't know what took over me, but I just did it. It was risk I was willing to take and in the end, it paid off. There we sat embraced in a kiss as the sunset. I'm sure that anyone who may have walked by and saw us would have thought that they were watching a movie. It was just the perfect scene. Everything fit so well together. My heart was skipping and my stomach was doing loopy loops. I was just so happy. I didn't want it to end. It did, though, and Sarah and I just sat there and looked at each other and smiled.

We walked back into the hotel together. I think that if my face were any redder it would have looked like I had an apple for a head. I also couldn't stop smiling. You know that feeling you get when you get something you thought you would never get. Well picture how much bigger that feeling would be if that thing you thought you would never get was the love of the one you cared for more than anything in the world. I didn't want the moment to end. I just wanted time to stop and stay right there with her and me standing there forever.

I walked Sarah up to her hotel room. We stood there for a minute or two just looking at each other. Finally she gave me a hug and she was gone. I had to hold on to the railing as I made my way to my hotel room. My legs were so shaky I could barely stand. I walked into my room and dropped down on the bed and just stared up at the ceiling. Was this for real or was it just a dream?

I felt my lips and knew it was for real. I turned and looked out the window. Suddenly I jumped up and let out cheer of joy. I felt like such an idiot, but it didn't matter. It was the happiest I had been since Seth's accident. I reached into my pocket and pulled out Seth's picture. I had kept one there since the accident.

I looked at it and said, "Well buddy it finally happened. I got her. The girl I thought I would never have I finally have. I wish you were here to see it."

I began to think and smiled. "Then again," I thought, "maybe you were there." I remembered that feeling I had that lead me to Sarah that night at the party. Seth always said he'd watch my back and maybe he was still doing that.

The rest of the trip didn't really matter to me as I spent most of it with Sarah. We went everywhere together and I couldn't be any happier. I always pictured it like that. I wouldn't have changed a thing. When we got back from the trip it was the same thing. We weren't exactly boyfriend and girlfriend. We might as well have been in the view of many. I took the chance and asked Sarah to go with me to our senior prom. She said yes and it was set. Almost nothing could have ruined it for me. Well, almost.

It was the night of the prom. I was getting ready. I decided to wear a black tux with a red vest covering my white shirt. I wore a black top hat. Sarah thought it would be pretty funny if I wore that with the outfit so I decided to do that. I was driving there in my car and I was picking up Ron and his girlfriend Jody before heading over to get Sarah at her house.

I drove over and picked up Ron and Jody and then we headed up to Sarah's house.

"Nice hat Jak," Ron joked.

"Yeah," Jody said with a chuckle.

"You want a ride," I asked. "Then shut up! Besides, Sarah thought it would be pretty funny if I wore it."

"You've gotten quite sweet on her haven't you," Jody declared.

"I guess I have," I said with a smile.

We finally made it to Sarah's house.

"Now you two behave while I'm gone," I warned. Ron snapped his fingers in disappointment. I walked up to the door and knocked. I could hear Sarah's parents arguing.

Finally the door opened and Sarah's dad was standing there. "What do you want," he snapped.

"I'm here to pick up Sarah," I replied.

"What for?" he asked.

"The prom Mr. Holland," I responded.

"Tonight is the prom?' Mr. Holland exclaimed.

"Of course it is," Mrs. Holland barked from the back room. "Why the hell else do you think she came down wearing that stupid dress?"

"Was that why she was asking me what I thought?" Mr. Holland exclaimed. "Oh well, she is up in her room. Just go up and get her."

I entered the house and all I really wanted to do was nail both of Sarah's parents in the face. I couldn't see how a parent, let alone both of them, could treat their child the way they treated Sarah. They never really paid attention to her. I sometimes wondered if they even cared about her. It was sad how that worked?

I made my way up the stairs towards Sarah's room. The radio was on. I knocked on the door.

"Sarah," I said, "it's time to go."

There was no reply. I figured she couldn't hear over the radio so I knocked again.

"You okay Sarah," I asked.

Still there was no reply.

"I'm coming in," I said.

I turned the doorknob and slowly opened the door.

"It's okay really. You know your parents are assholes. I'm sure you look…"

I never finished my sentence. I just couldn't. I slowly backed out of the room back into the wall in the hallway and slowly slid down it on my back. I stayed there motionless and rocked back and forth.

After a while Ron came up the stairs. "What the hell it taking so long," he snapped. "What the hell is wrong with you?" Ron turned and looked into Sarah's room. "Oh my God," he exclaimed. He ran down stairs and called 911.

As the paramedics took Sarah's body away I just sat there in the hallway, motionless. She had taken a gun and shot herself in the head. Her parents didn't even know, and I even questioned if they even cared. Ron helped me out of the house and into my car.

"It's going to be okay man," he said.

I just sat there on the ride back home. What was going on? Why did she have to kill herself? I knew the answer, though. When you feel like you aren't loved, suicide seems like the doorway out of the pain of life. It's a scary thought to me. I didn't even see it coming, or maybe it was that I chose not to see it. I knew she felt alone, but I never thought she couldn't get over it. That made me think that maybe I wasn't really there for her when she needed me the most. That maybe I could have done so much more. I soon began to hate myself. That same feeling I got when Seth died returned only this time it was far worse.

The day of Sarah's funeral I hid from everyone else. I stood in the distance behind a tree until everyone had left. I slowly made my way up to the grave and stood there looking down at it. I was holding back from crying just like I always did. I was angry, but sad at the same time. The only question in my mind was why did this have to happen? The thing was that there was no real answer for it.

"Hi," I finally said. I really didn't know what to say. Words just started coming out though.

"You know I'm a bit disappointed. I thought you were stronger than that, but I guess I was wrong. Then again I was wrong about a lot of things. I should have been there for you more. I feel as if I failed you in some way. For that I am sorry. You know I think you were the first girl I ever truly liked. No, make that love. It wasn't because of your looks, though, you weren't that bad to look at either. No it was because you were you. No one could change you into what they wanted. You were you and you were beautiful because of that. No matter what they said you stayed true to yourself. I wish everyone were like that. With that strength came weakness and that's why I guess I'm standing over your grave instead of staring into your eyes."

I pause at this to try and stop from crying. It didn't help, as I could no longer succumb to it anymore.

Through the tears I continued.

"You know, you were one of a kind Sarah."

I pulled out a folded piece of paper. I unfolded it and began. "You know I wrote you something. It's not much, but it's the best I could do you know. It's a poem. I figured that since you like poems I'd write a special one just for you." I read the poem to her:

To A Girl Named Sarah

I live life one day at a time,
But when you are around time seems to stop.
I feel as stupid as a mime,
And so very far from the top.

Could this actually be love?
Or am I just one crazy fool?
I wish I had that extra push and shove,

To save you from drowning in that pool.

I feel like I lost a duel,
And I wish I could understand.
Instead of feeling like a government mule,
When I can't see you and hold your hand.

I cried every night,
Because I failed my promise that I made.
That for you I would fight,
And be right there where I stayed.

You didn't deserve that!
Especially from me.
But I failed you because I just sat,
To a girl named Sarah I'll make her see.

The sorrow I feel,
Deep within my heart.
That I couldn't help her heal,
With all that was tearing her apart.

I saw her hide in her own personal hut,
But I said nothing.
I just kept my mouth shut,
As you lived your life like that sad song you would sing.

As the world keeps turning,
Everything seems so fast.
But I keep learning,
That some things aren't meant to last.

For all that you did I'll give you one thing,
A kiss to show you how I feel.
That you were my everything,
And that this love is real.

To a girl named Sarah…

I just stood there when I was finished. I reached into my back pocket and pulled out a yellow flower. I laid the poem and flower on the grave. I then took a step back and realized I wasn't alone. Jess was standing behind me.

"Hey," I said.

"Hi," she replied. "I didn't see you during the service."

"Yeah," I replied back. "I just didn't really feel up to it."

"I know how you feel," she said. Jess walked over to me and patted me on the back. I looked at her and was amazed at what I saw. Jess was crying. I know it may not sound all that amazing to you, but you don't really know her that well. I never saw Jess give in to pain, but for the first time she was.

She turned and began walking away, but stopped. She turned to me and with a smile said, "You know I once told Sarah that they may forget what you said, but they will never forget how you made them feel. You go through life meeting people and not knowing what an impact they have had on you until you're faced with the fact that things are changing. Don't ever forget what people did for you and how much certain people could make you smile because those are the ones you'll miss the most."

Jess then turned and left. I never saw Jess again after graduation, but I never forgot what she said that day because they were so true and they still are today. Words sometimes are the strongest thing in the world and Jess' words were some of the strongest I had ever heard from someone.

I looked at the flower that I had laid on the grave and a thought came across my mind. People are in a way like flowers in a garden. We all want to be that special flower that is better than all the rest. We want to be the ones that will stand out from everyone else. The thing is that in doing this we all soon become very much alike. Soon we become these similar flowers in that giant garden. We look down on those other flowers that don't exactly follow the same *"growth"* or style as the rest of us. What many other people in the world don't realize is that those are the flowers that are more beautiful than all the rest. In a field of daisies they are the roses that make our garden look just that much more beautiful. So why is it that we crush those who make that garden so beautiful and special?

Sarah was one of those flowers, but the world crushed her. Now our garden is one beautiful flower short. Sad it may be, but there is nothing we can do about it. With the death of one flower comes the growth of others. So if you are crying when you hear this, or you feel sorry for me, all I can say is don't feel that way. Life sometimes throws your some bad curves and there's nothing you can do about it, but go on. I lost my dad, my best friend and now my first love. Yeah it may not have been fair, but if I just threw myself into a pit of depression it wouldn't have changed anything. If you loose someone it's going to be hard, but don't let it control your life. It only makes things harder. The ones you care about may be gone, but they are still with you in some way. All you have to do is stay strong. If not for yourself, then at least for them.

Indeed my world had crashed down on me, but I would somehow find a way to survive. The basic human instinct is to survive, and that's exactly what I decided to do. Through the pain and loss I grew. I became stronger to pain. Yet with that strength I became cold to the world. Without the pain I lost feeling. I became numb inside to everything around me. This anger and hate were all I that knew from that day on. I may have been alive, but on that day I died. Not just a physical death, but it was more of a mental death. I hated everyone and everything from that day on. I was sick of being this joke for pain. From that day on I made a promise to myself that I wouldn't feel anymore. I saw it as the only way that I didn't have to go through such pain again. As I grew older it all kind of became my way of life.

C H A P T E R 5

CAN'T BELIEVE

Where?

Where am I going?
Looking from the left to the right
Taking a step further into the dark
Until I'm completely out of sight
Dreaming that I was killed by a shark

Where are you going?
Running further away from me
Until I can only hear you cry
Standing there, wishing I could be
All you need until the day you die

Where are we going?
As we keep going further from the truth
Into the darkness we will go

When around our necks we have a noose
Why couldn't this all be one big show

Why are we alone?
Because that was our choice when we were mad
Now all we are is sad

Growing up is a way of life. Everything in the world goes through it. They just grow differently. For trees they get bigger and need more water and sun to survive. For animals we grow stronger and have a need for something. It could be food, water, love, knowledge or power. It could be anything, but for certain animals it's different. For humans I'd guess the thing we'd want would be power. By power I mean fame, money, or anything associated with the high life. What ever we associate with the word power we want so we can have power.

After graduating high school I headed to UCLA. Going to college I began seeing things in a new light. I wanted to be successful and to do that I was going to have to change my way of life. I got colder. I was a stone. The only thing that mattered to me was reaching my goals. I was going to reach them no matter what. By any means possible I was going to be successful. The only problem was that I didn't know what I wanted to be successful at. So as you can guess college really didn't go as smoothly as I had hoped or planned it to be.

I took a bunch of different classes hoping that maybe I'd fine something I'd like and then I could figure out what I really wanted to do. The problem with that was that I became swamped with work. So because of that work I really didn't get to hang out all that much as most kids do in college. I wanted to finish the work so that maybe I could get something from it. You know, like gain some knowledge and even respect for myself. My whole view of what was important to me you could say had changed from when I was in high school. I lost contact with all of my friends back home. Ron, Brad, Isaac, Andrew and everyone else were just these memories in my past. It wasn't that I had planned it out that way. It all just seemed to work out that way.

In college I had a few new friends that made things a little bit easier. It wasn't the same though. You know that feeling you get sometimes that tells you something isn't right. Well that's how it felt sometimes. It just felt like everything was fake, and nothing around me was really happening. It was all just one big dream and when I woke up I'd call Sarah and we'd hang out with Seth, Ron, Brad and everyone. We'd laugh and play around and I'd be smiling. Everything would be the way that it should have been. The thing was that it wasn't fake. This was real life and not some TV drama. I'd just have to find a way to survive. The way I chose was knowledge. By filling my mind with all these facts I figured that I could cope with everything around me and not have to face it.

So I strived to better my life. I did the work that my teachers gave me and I did the best job that I could. Things just seemed to make that much more sense to me. I wasn't as confused as I use to be when I was growing up. My teenage years were over, and out of that darkness that once covered me I wanted a man to come walking out. I was going to be strong and have a will to survive. A man, a word I never thought would have been associated in describing me.

I had finally found the path, that growing up, I had always tried to stray far away from. I just couldn't believe it though. I had come so far yet I lost so much. Was it really worth it? There was no real answer for that question. I had grown, but I had lost. Those loses I think sometimes seemed heavier than the things that I had gained. I had lost my dad, but I had gained strength. I had lost my best friend, but I had gained respect for others. I had lost my first love, but from that I had gained a stronger love for those I still had. I wasn't really able to think about that though. My time in college was taken up mostly by my college work. That was until something happened.

One night I found myself free of work and free to go out. I met with my friend Steve Mallard and Bruce Conners. Steve was the friendly giant, as long as you stayed on his good side at least. He stood at six seven at the least and had this nicely combed back blonde hair. Bruce was your average nice guy. He was interesting because he really broke that view that many girls have when they think of "guys." I think Bruce was more concerned about caring for a girl than their actual looks, not that every guy just looks at a girl's looks but it sometimes seems that way. Well I don't mean he was going out with ugly girls, but I mean more that if he could relate with a girl that would mean more to him than the actual looks of the girl. If the girl was hot then hey, it was an added bonus. I think Bruce was a good example to all of us guys. Sex isn't everything in life and he realized that. It's fun, but when it comes to the big picture of life, finding that special someone is more important than just a weekly booty call. That was my view any ways I guess.

Many people find it hard to find that special someone. It seems too hard to commit to a relationship. There's these kinds of fear of lose that can sometimes over whelms us. Love should defeat all those things that may block our paths to the one we love. Getting there may not be easy but many things in life aren't. It's really up to you to make that choice. We figure that love is just a word that we don't have to think all that much about. It's just a word in our lives that we throw around. We have to make a choice. Love or to forever be alone. You have to make that choice and tell the one you love what you choose. To love or not? It really does change everything doesn't it? So the question you must have to ask yourselves is what do I choose? I hope you all make the right choice or you will forever regret it.

Back to the story: Steve, Bruce and I went to this party. I was a bit skeptical about going, but I figured I deserve to have fun for one night. I hadn't really been out in the couple of months I had been up in college because of my class work. We arrived and it was just like being back home. The keg was out and smoke filled the air. Yep, just like home. Steve introduced me to some of his friends. I got myself a seat and just chilled and watched the party. I really didn't feel much like drinking that night. I just wanted to chill. You know, take it easy and sit back. Take in the nightlife and see things from a sober point of view for once. Something I never really did back home.

The party went on and I went around talking to people and meeting some for the first time. I decided to go out for a smoke real quick. I usually didn't smoke cigarettes all that much, but I just felt like I needed one to calm me down. I walked out the door and sat on the steps. The streets were pretty clear and everything was quite calm. In fact things seemed too calm I remembered. I suddenly got one of those bad feelings I usually got right before something bad happened. That feeling soon turned to fear as I saw three to five police cars zoom up to the front of the house. I quickly ran into the house. "Cops," I yelled. Everyone was too trashed to pay attention to me. I was about to yell again when the door was knocked down. One cop quickly brought me to the ground and others grabbed any kid they could.

I spent the night in a jail cell that night. I was cleared of any charges since I was clean and so was Bruce. Steve wasn't as lucky though and was put on probation, which was a lot better than what some of the others were getting. Apparently a neighbor had tipped off the cops and since there was pot and some of the kids that were drinking weren't twenty-one. Everyone was pretty screwed over. I thought I'd be okay, but the school found out about the whole incident and as an example to any future incidents I was expelled. I thought it was the biggest load of crap and as you can guess I was pretty pissed off. I tried to fight the decision, but ultimately it was to no avail and the expulsion stood. There was nothing I could do about it, but just deal with the whole thing. My days of trying to expand my knowledge were cut off.

I had no choice but to return home and get some jobs to try and build up some money. I was hoping that if I saved up enough money I could buy an apartment so that my mom didn't have to watch me. She was getting old and the last thing she needed was to worry about someone like me. I knew that my mom deserved better than that and I was going to try and do that for her.

The only person I really had to hang out with was Brad. He had bought an apartment in town and was working at a bar. Ron and everyone else were either in college or had moved away. It was okay though because I finally got a chance to just chill with Brad. It used to always be Seth, Brad and me just hanging out and shooting the breeze. After the accident Brad and I never really hung out with each other all that much. I guess that when we both saw the other we remembered Seth. So we really didn't hang out all that much.

Brad got me a job at the bar he was working at and we bartended together there. It was an interesting job if anything else. As expected I saw my fair share of drunken people while working there. The thing is that usually one of those drunken people was Brad. Brad was really developing a drinking problem. It all came to a head though one night when Brad's ex girlfriend decided come to the bar with her new boyfriend.

We were working one night when she came walking in with her new boyfriend. They walked right over to the bar and sat there looking at Brad.

"Hey brad," she snickered.

"Hi, Autumn," Brad said avoiding any eye contact with her.

Autumn just smiled and put her arms around her boyfriend.

"This is Dan. He's my *new* boyfriend," she snickered with a smile. "He really knows how to treat a lady. Unlike some people I know."

"Don't you mean dog?" Brad snapped.

Autumn's boyfriend stood up at this.

"What'd you say, prick?" he barked.

Brad, still avoiding any eye contact by looking through the supply of alcohol behind the bar answered, "I said that's one stupid bitch on your arm there."

Before Autumn's boyfriend could react to this Brad pulled out a bottle and bashed it over the guy's head. Brad then jumped over the counter and attacked the guy. Soon the fight was broken up and the cops are called. Brad was escorted out of the bar in handcuffs. This Dan guy was spared from that as he was taken to the hospital for stitches. Brad was fired from the bar of course and I was fired as well being that I was a friend of Brad. I'm guessing that the owner of the bar didn't want to have a reoccurrence of the whole incident. I never really understood the logic of firing me though. I guess he figured I'd be like Brad. It didn't matter really.

Brad soon left and headed into the city to search for what he called "his true calling." I never knew what it was though. All I knew was that once again I was alone and struggling to get money to help my mom out. She was getting pretty sick and I needed money for all of her medical bills. All those years of drinking were finally catching up to her I'm guessing. I had to keep liquor away from her for fear that if she did drink her liver would just curl up into a little ball and die. She was all that I had left at the time. Amazing being that I was only twenty-four at the time and I still had a lot of life left to live.

Like all things, some things must come to an end. On March 28, 2015, my mom, Linda P. Davis, died at age fifty-six. She died in her sleep at the hospital when she was getting a check up. The funeral was fairly easy for me if you can believe that. I had been too far to many funerals in my time, but this one was the one that really affected me. My mom had left me the house and a good amount of money was collected from her life insurance. I paid off the house and my car. I got myself a job in a newspaper office. I was a reporter I guess you can say. I only took the small stories, but it really didn't matter to me. It was a paycheck and I needed the money in any way that I could get it.

The house really didn't feel the same anymore. It was…quiet. I can't say that I didn't mind the quiet all that much, but it just didn't feel the same. You know how when we are growing up we always picture how it's going to be when we are taking care of ourselves. We can do this and that and no one can tell us not to do it, well except maybe the police. The thing was that now that I was back in the house that I spent most of my life in all I wanted was for things to go back to the way they were before. I wanted things to be…normal again.

I walked into my mom's room. I made the bed and shut the door for the last time. That room was hers and it was always going to be hers. I walked around the whole house then and all these memories of my life in the house poured into my mind. Sitting and eating dinner with my mom at night. Sitting on the couch where Seth, Brad, Ron and I would usually sit and watch TV or talk about our plans for that night. There was the clock that Isaac ran into when trying to avoid the water balloon that I had thrown at him one summer. Then there was the hole that I had to plaster up after Seth tripped and fell into the wall when he was drunk.

All these things and so much more had happened in this house. To think that at one time I wanted to leave it. Yet, somehow in some screwed up way fate kept me right there. I spent the rest of my life in that house. My life began in that house and it would end there as well. The funny thing is that looking back I wouldn't have had it any other way.

The days it was sunny everything just seemed to be all right. It was like nothing could go wrong. My friends and I would just walk. We'd walk all around town and talk. It didn't matter if we felt sick, sad, angry or anything else. When we walked everything just seemed great, period. At least to me any way. I know I said I lost my family before, but having my friends around seemed to make everything better. In fact if you were to ask me the names of my family I couldn't give you one or two names. I'd have to give all the names of those who I cared about with all my heart, my friends. I cared for my family, but you know that old saying "blood is thicker than water?" That just didn't seem to work for me. My family was there for me, but I sometimes felt like they only did it because they felt they had to, not because they cared about me. With my friends and me, just looking into ours eyes you could tell and see the love and compassion that we all shared for each other. If one of us were hurting we all were hurting. You can't put a price on that.

Brad was the last friend I had so he was very important to me. I lost a lot of friends. Whether because of death or because of the fact that we grew apart from each other, I had lost them. I really didn't want to loose Brad. That's why I made up my mind and headed into the city to find him and to see how he was doing. I would never forget that day.

It was July 9, 2020. It was a warm summer's day. I drove up into Manhattan to the apartment building where I was told Brad was staying. It was a scruffy building which to tell you the truth didn't surprise me all that much. I went up to Brad's apartment and knocked on the door. There was no reply. I knocked on the door a couple more times. "You looking for Brad?" a voice asked from behind me.

I turned and saw that it was a small skinny Hispanic man.

"Yeah," I answered. "Do you know if he's in?"

"He's not in," the man replied.

"Do you happen to know when he will be in?" I asked.

The man shook his head and said, "He's not coming back."

A fear took over me.

"Is he okay?" I questioned.

"He's fine," the man replied. The fear was lifted.

"He didn't pay his rent for the past few months. So being that I'm the landlord I had no choice but to kick him out. Your friend is probably in his car somewhere."

The man turned and headed down the hallway. What actually shocked me was that I once again I wasn't all that surprised. Brad usually was lazy when it came to important things so this was just like him to slip up on his rent.

I headed back to my car and began to drive in search of my friend. It took all day, but finally around 10:50 P.M. I found his car. I walked over to the car and there lying in the back seat was Brad. I knocked on the window.

"Hey, Brad, wakey, wakey," I yelled.

Brad shuffled in side the car, but finally lifted his head and stared at me in deep confusion. I don't think he was expecting to see me.

"Jak?" he stammered.

"The one and only," I laughed. Brad got out of the car and we shook hands. "I see you smell the same as I remember you."

"Funny," Brad said. "You know it's not easy to take a shower when you're out of work and a house."

"I would guess not," I said. "So I'm guessing your search for your "calling" isn't going all that well?"

"Not exactly," Brad replied.

"So what happened," I asked.

Brad and I sat on the curb and just talked about everything that had happened. Apparently Brad had started hanging out with a pretty bad crowd and his drinking habit wasn't helping matters. He was in a lot of debt and eventually it all caught up to him. When we were done I just looked at him and said, "You know you can always stay with me if you needed to. I have plenty of space in my house."

"That's okay," Brad said. "I'll be okay. Besides I've got this job lined up that's gonna change everything."

"What kind of job is that," I questioned.

"I can't tell you," Brad said looking away.

"Look, don't get yourself in trouble," I warned.

"Don't worry about me," Brad quickly said. "I'll be okay.

With that we shook hands and hugged. Then I was off. The next time I would see Brad would be on the news. Apparently this "job" he was talking about how it was going to change everything did change everything. Brad and a couple of others tried to rob a bank. He was lucky in that he wasn't shot. He was put on trial and sentenced to life in prison. I visited him as much as I could until the day he died. With Brad's death I had official lost the last of my old friends.

Brad wasn't the last person to have entered my life and then leave. No the last person was Amanda Pontone. I had met Amanda in college and after I was expelled we still kept in touch. She was the only girl after Sarah that I actually saw myself being with, but there was one major problem with that. She was in California and I was in New York. You see the problem. Yeah so the only contact we had with each other was the phone, email, and instant messenger. It was good and all, but I wanted more. That's understandable right? You really can't start something with someone when they are on the opposite coast.

That all changed when she graduated though. She bought a house up in New York, only a couple of miles from my house and started her teaching career. We would meet every weekend and hang out. I started getting that same feeling that I had gotten when I was around Sarah, and I liked it. I had finally found another person that I could care about. Then again maybe I cared too much about her. We had gotten pretty close like I said and yes we had had sex with each other a couple of times. Then something happened that I wasn't really prepared for.

It was a Monday morning when I got the call. I answered the phone and it was Amanda. I was a bit surprise to hear from her since it was already time for school to start. So I figured that she would be at work. She sounded a little bit worried on the phone. "What's a matter?" I asked. "Is something up? You know you can tell me anything?"

"I'm…" she started, "I'm late."

"Yeah I know," I responded. "School started a couple of hours ago."

"No," she replied. "I mean I'm *late.*"

It all suddenly clicked.

"You mean…" I started.

"Yes," she answered. My mind was spinning. Could she actually, no she couldn't. Then again, could she?

"Have you taken a test?" I asked.

"I'm about to do that now," she replied. "I'm scared."

"I'll be over there in a little bit," I declared. "Then we can do it together.

I quickly got dressed and called in a sick day to work. Then I was out the door, into my car and headed over to Amanda's place. When I pulled up she was already sitting outside on her front steps. I ran up and she just looked at me. She then handed me the test and I took a step back. It was positive.

I sat down next to her and put my arm around her.

"I want you to know," I began, "that I'm going to be there for you and our child." She hugged me. For the next nine months I spent most of the day over at Amanda's helping her out around the house. I still couldn't believe that I was actually going to be a father. Never in my wildest dreams did I actually think that I would become a father. It was mind-boggling to me, but it was actually going to happen.

It all became reality on December 8, 2021. On that day my son, Warren Thomas Davis, was born. He was a beautiful baby boy and it came to the point that the doctor almost had to threaten me to actually put him down. It's an amazing feeling when you hold your newborn baby for the first time. It's one of the greatest feelings in the world. I just wanted time to freeze for a little longer as I stared at his little body and his tiny hands gripped my fingers. Amanda moved in with me and we started to raise our son together. That was until he was two years old.

One day I decided to take Thomas to the park so that he could experience nature for a little bit. I was in a great mood that day. That was until I got home. Thomas had fallen asleep on the ride back so I was quiet when I entered the house. I whispered, "Amanda, you here." There was no reply, but I could hear movement. It was coming from my mom's room. I put Thomas down and made my way over. I opened the door and jumped back at what I saw. Right there in my mom's bed Amanda and another man were having sex. I shut the door quickly and walked out of the hallway.

Amanda came running out with a sheet rapped around her.

"Jak, it's not what you think," she exclaims.

"Then what the hell was it?" I snapped. "Was he helping you find a contact in my dead mother's bed? Is that it? Why the hell would you do that to me damn it? Why?"

"Jak calm down," Amanda asked.

"You were cheating on me," I snapped. "God only knows for how long you've been cheating on me."

Amanda looks to the ground.

"Well, how long has this been going on?"

"Four years," she answered.

"Four years!" I exclaimed. "You mean even before our son you've been cheating on me?"

"He might not be yours," she said still looking down.

"What did you say?" I asked in shock.

"He might not be yours," she repeated. I pulled a chair over to sit in before I fell to the floor. The son I had been raising for two years, the son I saw being born, and the son I had loved for the past two years in fact may not even be mine.

"I'm sorry," Amanda said.

"I want a paternity test," I declared, "and I want you out of my house."

A week later we had the paternity test. It was a nerve wrecking experience for me. I just kept rocking back and forth until I had the results. In the end Thomas Warren Davis wasn't my son. Amanda took full custody of him and I never saw her or Thomas again. As I walked up the steps to my house I pulled out something I had kept in my pocket since the day I caught Amanda cheating on me. On the way back from the park with Thomas I had stopped at a store. Not just any store though. It was a ring store. With the money that I had saved up I had bought a ring. I had planned to propose to Amanda that day. I wanted to be in her and Thomas's lives forever. As you can tell things didn't really work out that way.

I pulled out the ring and looked at it. It was a beautiful ring with a heart-shaped diamond in the middle. I had pictured her to say I do, but it didn't happen. I just stood there on the step looking at the ring. Finally I put my key in the door and opened it. I walked in and headed to the kitchen. I opened the garbage and dropped the ring in it. I had no use for it anymore unfortunately. I realized that it was official then. I was truly alone in the world.

Not only did I lose a love, but also I lost my heart and will to go on. There is nothing more painful than losing a child. That's why parents always try and shelter their children. They care way too much for them, but that's what makes them parents. I wasn't a parent anymore though. That was taken from me and I wasn't quite ready for that. Everything from my past was gone and now everything that I wanted for my future was gone. I was the lone soldier, left to fight the battle alone. Walking that empty road of loneliness is a hard route to take, but I was taking it I knew I wasn't going to win, but I had to keep fighting for all those soldiers who died before and all that would follow. I had to keep going on.

Chapter 6

The End

An Unhappy End

This is the end of everything we had
Nothing is left but this unhappiness
I'm crying, wishing I wasn't so sad
I'm hiding the sorrow from emptiness

This is my end and I can't go back
Can not change that which has already pass
Will not focus on that which I do lack
The engine is empty, there's no more gas

Reliving the past hurts me dearly now
But yet I'm not feeling any real pain
Don't give me that look or make any sound
I'm not crazy, I'm not even insane

I'm telling you this cause you are my friend
Leaving now, because this is my unhappy end

Have you ever heard the phrase, "You never really know what you have until it's gone"? I've heard it plenty of times, but I never really paid all that much attention to it. Not many people do I think? Then it happens. That very quote becomes your reality. There's nothing you can do to stop it I guess. You're basically stuck. I guess that's what happened to me. I never thought much about my life. To me there wasn't much to think about that's why. I never was the jock or Mr. Popular. I never went out with the prom queen, or anyone for that matter. I never won a major award, nor had the people around me show me the respect that others and myself longed to have one day.

In fact, I just watched life pass me by day by day. Life, ha, never thought much about my life and where it was heading. Now suddenly, as it disappears right in front of me, it's all I can think about. Everything I once had and could have had is now going to be just another sad and distant memory that I can't get back. It really makes me believe that maybe I should have paid more attention to my life instead of ignoring it the way that I did.

You see that happens when you're facing death my friend, if you don't mind me calling you my friend. You see when you know your world is all coming to an end all you can think about is not what is going to happen, but what has already happened. You remember everything from when you were born, to your first bike, to your first kiss, and everything up to the point where you realized it was all going to come to an end. You become saddened with the thought that there really aren't going to be any more memories, and that the memories you already have are the last memories you got. They're all that you have left, and all that you will ever have. So all you can do really is smile. It's all you can really do to hide the pain.

I know it may sound a bit crazy to you, heck maybe even a bit scary, but you really don't know this for your self until it actually happens to you. When you have no control of what happens to you then you will realize it. What can you do, though? You can't go back in time and fix your life up so that when that day actually came you would have no regrets. No, unfortunately it doesn't work out that way. All you can do is remember all of the things you did and wanted to do. They may seem so close, but the fact of the matter is that they are so far away and are drifting furthering away as we get older. Our memories drift away because as we get older we just forget about them and turn our focus more on the present. Maybe we should have paid more attention to our past instead of the present when we grew older. Maybe then we could improve our present. No one does that, though. It's mostly because the present is right there in front of us, and the past is, well, the past.

It's the curse of being human I guess. We're such an advanced species. We have achieved all these amazing things that we've created and all these things we can now do. We assume that all the animals are jealous of us. After all we have the thumb. No, I have a different view. See when an animal dies I believe that they don't think all that much about their lives. They realize that this it and that then they're dead. It's not one of those Disney cartoons where they basically make this big dramatic scene in which even the most macho man would cry. No, they just wait for their cruel fate that has been drawn for them. Not us humans though. Our minds just begin working like they never had before and our memories just begin pouring into our heads. I think it is because so many of us fear death that we don't want it to come and when it does come, we try and hold on for as long as we can. That's what makes our deaths harder than an animal's death I say. I hope that in some way all that I have said may have helped you in some way. I always wished that I could have helped in some way those with problems in their lives. I couldn't though because I was too consumed with my own problems to really care. That's the problem with most people. We are too focused on ourselves to realize all of the hurt that is happening all around us from day to day. Whether it be war, death, love or anything, if it doesn't affect us then it really isn't important enough to worry about.

You see we owe it to those around us and ourselves to not be that way. We have to fight that common idea of life. When you care about someone other than yourself you not only help them but you help yourself. You can discover so much about yourself when you do that. Maybe even things you may not have realized before. It can be scary but the benefits that come from it are worth it. Believe me when I tell you this. When you care for others you care for yourself.

After Brad died I lived my life in solitude from the world. I thought that by hiding from the world I wouldn't be consumed by it. The thing is that there really isn't any way that you can avoid the world. Everything we do in our lives is in some way affected by the world. I mean look at the clothes you are wearing right now. I'm betting that in some way TV, school, friends, family or maybe even love, in some ways, determines what you are wearing. You just might not realize it, but if you really think about it you will.

You can deny it, but that's just how it works. If you are a businessperson you probably wear a suit and tie or something very nice and dressed up. Why? Well the reason is that that is what is expected from you. If you listen to rap you probably wear baggy pants, long shorts or you wear your pants half way down your backside. You probably also have a designer label on like FUBU or Phat Farm or some other label.

It's because that's the style associated with your group. If you skate you have the skater shoes and maybe even grow your hair out. We are all controlled by the world. Our talk, our language, our personalities and anything that we do are effect by the world and how it states how we should act. Maybe I'm wrong and you don't believe this applies to you. Well then I'm wrong, but I'm betting that most people would agree or at least realize that what I'm saying is true. When we do that we not only betray ourselves, but we betray those around us. The thing is that we do it everyday without seeing how much we have changed since we were young.

We all change. Some of us change more than others but we all change in our own ways. We must never forget who we are and always should be.

Like Jess said, "they may forget what you said, but they will never forget how you made them feel. You go through life meeting people and not knowing what an impact they have had on you until you're faced with the fact that things are changing. Don't ever forget what people did for you and how much certain people could make you smile because those are the ones you'll miss the most." Read that last part again. Isn't that true? If there is anything you get from this remember that.

We have to remember that. We impact all those around us. The things we have to decide is whether we want to be remembered as the person that made those around them feel better or the asshole who didn't care about anyone but themselves. We have to decide that before it's too late because the clock is ticking. We don't live forever and neither do those around us. You never know when it's going to end so you have to act quickly.

Like a scout always says, "be prepared." Only then will life seem just that much easier.

People die and people live. It's just the way things work out in this world. There's nothing you can do to control that. All you are able to do is cherish the time you have with those you care most about. You never know how much longer you have with them. Nothing is certain in life but if you love and care for others life just seems to make all that much more sense. Don't waste the years you have left on this world alone and cold. When you do that you leave all those you care about behind. Some people might say you mean nothing and you will always mean nothing. Maybe you do, but the only way that can ever happen is if you choose to. If you let those people get to you and change you then yes, you are nothing.

You have to stand tall and be able to say, "No, I mean something."

It's up to you to choose how you want your life and how you affect those around you. Make sure that you make the right choice and stand tall with the confidence of knowing you mean something.

I may not know much about life, but no one really does. It's one of those mysteries that I believe we will never truly understand until after we are actually dead and have lost life. It doesn't sound all that fair does it? I'd have to agree with you on that. Probably if we had that answer people in the world wouldn't be as screwed up as they are now. We'd know what we have to do and we'd do it because it would be this clear straight path. The thing is that it wasn't set up that way. If God, or if you don't believe in God then whatever is watching over us, wanted it to be that way then they would have done it a long time ago. So you just have to deal with it.

My favorite saying to people was "smile to hide the pain." I loved saying that cause there were so many people like that when I was growing up and even now. The years may go by, but some things just never change. One of those things is people hiding their fears and sorrow. I'd tell those people to just open up and say what they feel, but then again

I really couldn't do that myself. You see I was once exactly like them and I know how hard it is. That feeling that you mean nothing and that no one in the world really cares about what makes you cry yourself to sleep. So I won't tell you to open up if you don't want to. What I will tell you, though, is that you have to find a way to stay strong because when you do that then, and only then, can you one day beat that fear.

I know what I'm saying may have come out of nowhere, but allow me to explain why I tell you this. You see a couple years ago I was driving home from a bar. I was highly intoxicated and was speeding down the rainy high way. Perhaps I shouldn't have been driving, but for some reason I didn't seem to care. I didn't care about anything any more really. The music on radio screamed out at me as stared out into the dark stormy night. Fear, I had no fear. Everything was on my terms and my terms alone.

Rain hit the windshield like the sound of firecrackers. I could feel the car slipping a little on the high way, but I pushed on. All that was running through my mind was everything that I just told you. All the joy, sorrow, pain, an all those emotions I had faced were pouring down on me. The faster I drove, the more it seemed as if I was running away from them. I could feel myself slowly lose control of the car. It's also interesting how whenever you seem to run away from your emotions, the more trapped you are with them. They always catch up with you. In my case it came in the form of a guard rail in which I crashed through.

My car slammed hard into the guardrail and soon I found myself trapped with in my car as it rolled down a hill. Some call my lucky because my car slammed into a tree. You see if not for that my car would have fallen off the edge of a cliff into a stream down below. If you ask me, I don't really know if I was lucky or not.

By the time the fire department got to the scene I was on the verge of just giving up. They had to cut the car up pretty good just to get to me. Careful was the name of the game since any false movement could end with the car sliding of or me dying just from the shape I was in already. They finally got me up the hill to a helicopter to be flown to the near by hospital.

I can't really tell you the scene all that well, for you see I was in a complete daze. Everything moved almost dream like. Everything appeared so slowly and unreal like that at times I did question reality itself.

Being rolled into that emergency room the only thing I heard was the doctor say, "I don't know if he's going to make it?"

That's all that was ringing through my head. I knew then I had to decide whether to fight for my life or not.

From what I was told I technically dead on that table for a minute while the doctors and nurses fought to bring me back. I believe it was in this minute that something happened to me. You always hear stories of that bright white light. To me, there was no such thing really. All I could see was myself on that table. Beaten and broken are possible the best way to describe my appearance. Yet for some reason I didn't feel alone. All I could look at, though, was myself so I had no clue as to who was beside me. I suddenly felt myself pushed towards my body. As I turned I looked up into a void of light. There was a figure standing within it waving back at me, it was Seth.

It'd be three days before I awoke from my comma. The doctor said they thought for sure that I was going to die right there on the table, but when the clock struck midnight my pulse had returned. I sat in silence at this. You see, when it struck midnight it had been exactly sixteen years since Seth's accident. Seth was sixteen when he died. I didn't tell the doctor this though for fear that he'd believe me to have suffered damage to my brain. I just laid in silence and thought.

It'd be couple of weeks before I was finally released from the hospital, but it was a humbling experience. I had to work hard to recover from my injuries. Walking was an especially difficult task, yet I had to endure. When I finally returned home I began working on the story you have before you today, in hopes of reaching out to others just like me, because perhaps if we all share our knowledge and trials with each other then maybe we can help each get through them.

Seth gave me a philosophy to live by.

He told me, "Live fucking life bro, because it's going to end one way or another and you don't know when your clock is up. It's a bunch of BS, but we don't make the rules. We just go about this crazy game of life with no real idea of when it's all going to end. You see all these faces every day, and sometimes you don't even know how many are going to be there when you wake up. The sad thing is that we all take it for granted. We believe everything is going to be alright, that nothing bad can happen to us. The truth is, though, that you could be walking down the street and BAM, some asshole in a BMW hits you because he's driving too fast. Then all that is left is those shattered memories. You don't know what the future holds, so why not work on the present? At least if you do that then you can leave this world with a smile on your face. We don't know what the future has in stored for us, but it's better to be safe then sorry."

There really isn't anything left for me to say I guess. So as I fade away I'll leave you with this. Never let anyone change your life. That belongs to you and you alone. Yes, this may be my story and you may have liked it or you may have not liked it. The bottom line is that this is my story. You yourselves are creating a story of your own every day you wake up and enter the world around you. You just might not be telling people about it. Everything you do, say and go through creates that story even if you don't think it does. So you have just one more choice to make. You have to decide how you want your story to be. You can make it happy, sad, scary, and interesting or you can just make it dull. I would have to guess that we all want our stories to be great. You have to ask yourself, though, how am I going to make my story great?

Either way you look at it, though, this is my story and I'd like to thank you for listening to it. My name is Jak and just like you I am, and will always just be, "Just Another Kid."

A Simple Smile

A simple smile is all it will take
Nothing else is really needed today
In this world we will make a mistake
There is nothing we really have to say

A simple smile is all we will see
The pain may grow but we will all survive
Where there is happiness we will not flee
Deep inside you will always be alive

A simple smile is all I will need
Just to see you happy with no more pain
It's just a small thing, almost like a seed
Go and look around for a single name

So go outside and walk or drive a mile
Find someone and give them a simple smile

THE END

978-0-595-78819-4
0-595-78819-X

Printed in the United States
45756LVS00004B/16

9 780595 788194